Peace at Any Price

Jim Hunter and Matt Harrison's Double H ranch thrived . . . till their crew marched away to war's glory, and they were ruined by outlaws who burned them out and murdered the last man on the payroll, harmless oldster Walt Burridge.

When the war ended, the two H's started over. But for Jim war and the Reconstruction had wrought changes beyond endurance. His former sweetheart, pretty Alice Cornhill, had been claimed by another. So Jim rode out and into the arms of his wartime love, the gun-running adventuress Lena-Marie Baptiste.

There, he was quickly trapped by his vow to avenge Old Walt. How would he choose between enmity and love, life and death?

Peace at Any Price

CHAP O'KEEFE

A Black Horse Western

ROBERT HALE · LONDON

© Chap O'Keefe 2007
First published in Great Britain 2007

ISBN 978-0-7090-8269-9

Robert Hale Limited
Clerkenwell House
Clerkenwell Green
London EC1R 0HT

www.halebooks.com

Typeset by
Derek Doyle & Associates, Shaw Heath
Printed and bound in Great Britain by
Antony Rowe Limited, Wiltshire

1

BLACK NIGHT ON THE DOUBLE H

The two H's, Jim Hunter and Matt Harrison, hazed the remnants of a once fair-sized herd of cattle on to the best of the Double H pasture. Here the grass was long and dry, a short ride over scrub-clad knolls from ranch headquarters.

'We can't afford to let Border scum get away with these cows,' Matt said.

Of sandy colouring, thirty-some years of age, and by a few the senior of the pair, he was hot and tired after rounding up the straying critters from a ten-acre lot of dense brush. But he was also a prudent, hard-working man, averse to needless risk and loath to witness the disintegration of his and Jim's fortunes.

Jim had a less sober, more accommodating approach to the undeniable blows life had handed out. He shrugged. 'Anything could happen, Matt.'

Since the nation had descended into civil war, the Double H had been going downhill. Before the hostilities, it had been the best cattle outfit in the Trinity Creek country. Now the two partners had their backs to the wall.

The War Between the States had at first seemed distant and irrelevant. Texas Governor Sam Houston had stood loyally for the Union, but Justice Oran M. Roberts had called a secession convention which voted 166 to 8 to withdraw from it and, when Houston had refused to take the oath of allegiance to the Confederacy, he had been removed from office.

The political rumblings had made no difference in the day-to-day running of the Double H – till its men began riding away to theatres of war outside the state where the conflict raged.

It was a common story. A lack of able-bodied fellows willing to carry on working as cowpunchers left Jim and Matt struggling with no crew except one gimpy old-timer good only for cookhouse chores. Longhorns ran half-wild in the south Texas mesquite. Ranch buildings, corrals and fences were neglected. Paint blistered, boards warped and cracked, and nothing was replaced or refurbished.

'That's a result of no manpower, not mismanagement,' Jim told Matt, who was the more disconsolate about it. 'Two men can only do so much, however keen.'

Matt shook his head irritably. 'I can't abide seeing the place let go to hell. Secession was damnfool nonsense.'

'Well, there was kind of justification. It was ratified by popular vote, and you have to make allowances for the pull of the shooting and the glory.'

Sourness wasn't in Jim's nature. He had a more social, irrepressible personality. Something of a humorist and extrovert, he had a penchant for the vivid and flamboyant features of cowboy dress – the bright red bandanna, the high-crowned hat with fancy band, the tall-heeled, waxed-calf boots with coloured top binding and trim and a stitch pattern on the front of the leg. And he cottoned to living by his wits.

For five years, Jim had given the Double H some dash in its dealings with the world. He'd choose the precarious trail over the safer if it promised more profit or the spice of excitement. He was happy to leave it to his long-time friend Matt to supply the partnership venture with stability and security. Truth to tell, he was drawn by the Confederate cause.

But right now his business, and Matt's, was saving the Double H.

Sundown was near, the beef was settling contentedly to graze in the untrampled grass to which it had been driven, but the pair's work wasn't over. Though not in prime condition, the stock was the best their ailing business had left after successive raids by rustlers had denuded the Double H range of hundreds of head of cattle. The reduced herd had to be guarded round the clock.

The raiders struck at any hour. They were opportunists, hitting properties largely committed by their rash, war-gone owners to the care of womenfolk, old men and small boys.

'Figure we'll both be on nighthawk duty,' Jim said.

'Well, I reckon the owlhoots are more apt to work in the dark an' there ain't no second shift we can call on,' Matt said drily. 'Old Walt won't be expecting us back at the ranch house before daybreak.'

Walter Burridge was a veteran of the Mexican troubles. He'd been shot in the right leg while storming Santa Anna's army at San Jacinto. Helping secure the Lone Star Republic's independence had left him with a permanent limp. He'd become a drifter and a derelict, addicted to hard liquor.

Matt Harrison was often disappointed in the ways of humankind, finding his solace in the predictability of the animal kingdom. He worked well with dumb friends, particularly horses. It was this skill, harnessed with accurate knowledge of the country and ranch building, that had served him and Jim well in the late 1850s. But he was also compassionate to his less fortunate fellow-man and had rescued Old Walt from the brink of death with the offer of a home and employment.

Walt had stayed true to the brand when the rest of the Double H waddies had ridden off to war. 'I've had me a bellyful of soldierin',' Walt had said by way of self-exoneration.

At the side of a hole filled with the sweet water that irrigated the meadow where they'd bedded the cattle, Matt and Jim rested their mounts, set a small fire, ate a skimpy meal of jerky and corn biscuits, and drank hot coffee from tin mugs. They'd brought no bedrolls and made no camp.

The coffee was poor, bitter stuff – a wartime substitute produced from roasted acorns ground to a powder. Real coffee was hard to come by. Matt grimaced.

'Ugh! Scarce worth building a fire for this brew.'

Jim's habitual grin was wry. 'Best from McAuley's store in Trinity Creek. He blames the Yankee gunboats blockading the Gulf, and him a Unionist!'

Darkness came quickly and the range fell under the spell of night. Above the wild, trackless country that lay between this part of Texas and the sea, bright stars studded the clear sky. The air was scented by Drummond onion, with its white, purple-tinged flowers, and by the yellow evening primroses that clustered along the slopes.

Jim mounted up and quietly circled the herd. Peace seemed to stretch for endless miles every which way, till along about midnight it was broken by what sounded like a brief crackle of gunfire and its fainter echoes.

Jim joined Matt. 'What did you make of that?'

Matt looked puzzled. 'Hard to tell quite which direction it came from.'

'Could be a hunter. I seen white-tailed deer and Rio Grande turkeys hereabouts. Both favour them Mexican primrose leaves, and there's plenty around.'

But Matt's gaze was sweeping their horizons.

'A hunter? Don't think so,' he rapped. 'Look!'

A red disc of moon had risen above the knolls that hid the ranchers from the Double H. Smoke drifted across it, and when Jim sniffed he could smell the smoke, too, coming in over the night scents of the vegetation.

'The ranch!' he cried.

Together, they spurred their horses forward from the broad and luxuriant meadow. The gallop quickly brought them to the top of the obscuring elevation of the knolls.

They hauled up and stared. The home lot was spread moonlit before them: the stout ranch house, the big, weather-beaten barn, the unoccupied bunkhouse, the cookhouse, the water tank, the windmill and lesser structures huddled around the dusty, weed-edged yard.

The main house – long, low-running and slant-roofed – and most of the rest looked as shabby and sorry a sight as it did in better light, but nothing was as alarming as the barn.

A column of black smoke rose from the large structure which was lit redly from within by flickering flames.

Even as they yelled their anger and tore down on the scene, the flames leaped higher and sparks flew, threatening to ignite the other buildings. The smoke hung and spread into a dense, overhanging cloud.

At the edge of the yard, Jim and Matt's horses shied at the sight of the fire, their eyes rolling in terror. They would go no further. The partners flung themselves from their saddles.

'Where's Walt?' Jim asked.

Matt spotted the bucket, rolling on its side by the barn door, its load of water spilled.

'Hell! Maybe the crazy ol' galoot's gone in the barn!'

Jim ripped off his brightly coloured bandanna,

10

soaked it in the trough by the water pump and wrapped it round his face.

'I'll take a passear,' he said with forced lightness.

Boldly, he entered the murky, hot interior of the burning barn, crouching and groping around. At ground level, there was considerably more smoke than flame, which seemed concentrated in the hay loft. He found the old man stretched out on the floor, not far in.

With the fire raging and the loft floor and roof liable to fall in any moment, Jim had no time to check on Walt's condition. He could smell clothes and hair singeing, possibly his own as well as the prone man's. He grabbed Walt unceremoniously by the heels and dragged him out. Then the smoke got to him and he was racked with choking coughs.

Leaving Walt to Matt's inspection and care, Jim stumbled back to the trough and dunked his head.

'Aaah . . . I reckon I've lost my eyebrows. Is Walt gonna be all right?'

Straightening up, he was startled to see a lone figure burst from the abandoned bunkhouse, throwing aside an empty can. From the profile revealed in the moon- and firelight, he saw that the man was tall and powerful with a full black beard, straggly hair of the same colour and a distinctive hooked nose.

Jim shouted as the intruder ran for a horse they hadn't noticed before, hitched in the shadows of a clump of cottonwoods. His and Matt's broncs had bolted, but the factor that decided him to give no chase was a sudden whoosh as the bunkhouse exploded into oily flame. Instinctively, Jim grabbed

11

up another bucket and dipped it into the trough.

'That's no use!' Matt roared. 'You'll kill yourself. The place's dry as an old bone and soaked in lamp oil. Let it go!'

Jim tasted bile as the new fire took rapid, destructive hold and the arsonist made good his escape.

'All we can do is damp down the front of the house,' Matt said. 'See if we can prevent the flames spreading and save that. If this breeze picks up into a wind, it'll carry hot sparks from building to building.'

'But what about Walt Burridge?'

Matt's voice shook with emotion – grief, anger, Jim couldn't tell.

'We can do nothing for him. He's dead – shot dead! The bastards probably dragged him into the barn only to dispose of his body.'

Jim was shocked. 'Why do you thi—?'

But Matt didn't let him finish.

'No nevermind what I think for the moment!' he rasped. 'Let's just put our backs into saving what we can – fast!'

Tired though they were, they set to on the task of keeping fire from the ranch house that was their home.

It took a good hour before the danger passed. Then the blazes in the barn and bunkhouse burned themselves out. Both structures were gutted to blackened shells that collapsed into glowing heaps of ash, charred beams and twisted tin roofing. For most of the time, Jim kept his tongue still, saving his questions and concentrating on their fire-deterring efforts.

When Matt was satisfied the house would survive the catastrophe, and only smoke was left of the fires, drifting skywards and hanging over them, he went to rope a horse.

'Where to now?' Jim asked his purposeful comrade.

'Back to the meadow and the herd, though I've a hunch we'll find it gone.'

'You mean, you reckon—'

'I reckon every head of our last and best cows will be well away . . . good as across the Mexican Border already.'

And it was as Matt supposed. Topping the knolls on their return ride, they surveyed a grassy flat mockingly empty of stock. Their eyes pierced the pre-dawn darkness as far as it was possible and they sat their horses loosely, drained.

'Gone! The whole passel rustled – lock, stock and barrel. By daylight, they'll be over the river for sure and there won't be a goddamn thing we can do about it.'

Bitterly, unwashed faces blackened with soot, they figured the cunning of it. The marauders' true target had been the Double H's last few hundred head of fat cattle. The arson attack on the ranch buildings had been a feint, designed to draw Matt and Jim away from where they'd ridden sentry on their stock.

'Poor old Walt must have surprised them,' Jim surmised, 'put up a fight, and got himself murdered for his pains. That's the worst and cruellest part of the business, Matt.'

The hook-nosed man who had set the fire in the

bunkhouse had also burned his image into Jim's brain. Somehow, Jim had a gut feeling he would meet up with Hook-Nose again one day. He vowed to himself he would confirm Hook-Nose was a murderer, then kill him. Old Walt would be avenged.

Matt had never been so dispirited, so grim.

'After this, I give up. We've nothing left but the land and the house. Evil has its way in Texas. The Double H is busted to pieces. The fire was just the showdown. Howsoever you cut our loaf, there's no point starting over in these parts till the war is ended and some kind of law and order can be restored.'

'If we ain't going to fix things here, Matt, what will we do?'

'We'll shut and board up the house and look for work in Brownsville, though I'll understand if you don't want to come.' Matt allowed consideration to creep into his voice. 'I know you're sweet on Miss Alice Cornhill in Trinity Creek. . . .'

But Jim wouldn't hear of it. 'No, Matt, I'll go with you to Brownsville. I can send for Alice and her ma if we land on our feet.'

Texas, though not a major field of battle in the Civil War, supplied men and military material used elsewhere in the South. Most federal posts in Texas had been taken easily by the Confederates at the outbreak of fighting, but the Union Navy patrolled the Gulf. And the town of Brownsville, on the Rio Grande near the Mexican Border, had prospered from the federal gunboats' success in blockading most Southern ports.

Brownsville gave the Confederates an avenue though which they could ship cotton to Europe in return for ammunition, medicines, and other war supplies.

Jim agreed with Matt's strategy. 'Brownsville's the Confederacy's back door. It'll be a good place to wait out the struggle.'

The border town was a known hive of activity. Due to its location on the river, produce was transported to Brownsville and allegedly sold to Mexican companies. They moved it to Matamoros, across the river, then loaded it on to the ocean-going vessels bound for Europe.

But when Jim and Matt arrived in the bustling port, a shock awaited them that was to split their partnership and ultimately change the course of their lives.

2

THE BREAKUP

On the surface, Brownsville looked unchanged when Jim and Matt rode in to search the narrower, shady streets for a cheap lodging where they could board. Life was going on much as usual, reflecting the town's cosmopolitan character.

Many of the inhabitants had at some time lived in Mexico and had absorbed and practised Mexican custom. Brownsville's community of traders also included a large European contingent and Jim and Matt caught snatches of Spanish, French and German as well as English in a range of accents.

Men sat in saloons and cantinas, smoking and drinking. Dark-gowned women with baskets scuttled along on their way to market. People from the countryside were still carting in food despite the war, though probably not as much as the inhabitants could eat. A bell rang clangorously from a church's rectangular, gleaming white tower.

All this was in its place; what was out of place were the blue uniforms of federal soldiers!

'This looks bad, Matt,' Jim said.

Matt, who had a sneaking regard for the Northern forces and a leaning toward their politics, shrugged. He approached a bluecoat wearing a sergeant's stripes.

'We've just ridden in, Sergeant. What happened here?'

The sergeant was in good humour. 'Well, I hope yuh ain't a pair of Johnny Rebs huntin' trouble, fellers!' He laughed. 'I guess yuh wouldn't know – General Nathaniel P. Banks has marched in to close down illegal trade.'

'But this is Texas!' Jim objected. 'And Texans voted to quit the Union.'

The politics meant nothing to the sergeant.

'We had the greybacks outgunned, mister. They abandoned Fort Brown, blew it up with eight thousand pounds of explosives, and withdrew. If yuh'd bin in town, yuh'd've figured it was one of them earthquakes.'

Jim scowled. 'Why, that's real bad. Are you sure the Confederacy has moved out?'

'Would I josh yuh?' the sergeant said. 'Brownsville's now in the hands of the Union. If yuh're aimin' to stay, yuh better keep your guns in your holsters and make no trouble.'

'We ain't looking for trouble, Sergeant,' Matt said. 'We're looking for work.'

He pulled Jim away, fearing he might say something ill-advised.

The full gravity to themselves of the unexpected development soon became apparent when they found that, with much of the port's trade frozen, many stevedores were out of work and labouring jobs impossible to come by.

Walking the mean alleys near the wharf area dejectedly, they heard the beat of a drum and the bark of a loud voice. They turned a corner into a square to find a small crowd gathered around a Northern Army recruitment detail.

'Come on, boys! Step up and sign on to march to victory behind General Banks!'

'Overbearing Yankees!' Jim said under his breath.

But Matt took a contrary view. 'This damn war has gone on too long. I've had my fill of eating the dirt it's brung us. I'm joining up. Mebbe thataway I can make a mark.'

'By fighting for the Yankees? Count me out! If I stand by anybody in the mess, it's the South.'

At first, Jim thought Matt was acting on sudden impulse; that he wasn't completely serious. But he quickly realized otherwise and that, because Matt was Matt, the intention must have been forming silently in his mind for some time. Impetuosity wasn't in his nature.

He was devastated when Matt put his hand up to enlist.

'Well, if that's the way you really want to go, so long, Matt,' he said with vigour. 'You're in it on your own. See you when the fighting's over. I'd say the partnership's shelved for the duration.'

'I'm sorry we can't see eye to eye on this,' Matt said

stiffly. 'And I wish you well.'

So with surprising abruptness, they shook hands and split up, each man with his own thoughts, none of which was happy after their many years of shared toil, building up what had been the successful Double H cattle outfit.

Without any proper ceremony, a significant chapter in their lives closed.

Head bowed and heavy-footed, Jim took himself off in search of a saloon untainted by the new mood in Brownsville.

At a street corner, a man in Protestant clerical garb stood on a box berating a group that consisted mostly of bemused Mexicans. He was portraying the war for the Union in millennial terms and quoted the imagery of Revelation 20 from a tattered Bible, describing events near a prophesied close of history.

Jim vaguely recalled Matt having once asked him if he thought a Northern victory might prepare the way for the Kingdom of God on earth, as some preacher-men claimed in justification for sending their 'boys' off to war. He'd brushed off the question with some glib, oblique answer or other – 'I'm no great church-going feller, Matt' – conveying his uninterest. Maybe he'd made a mistake. . . .

'And I saw an angel come down from heaven, having the key of the bottomless pit and a great chain in his hand,' the gaunt-faced proselytizer was intoning. 'And he laid hold on the dragon, that old serpent, which is the Devil, and Satan, and bound him a thousand years. . . .'

'Bluebellies . . . sky-pilots, I don't cotton to either,'

Jim muttered, and turned through swinging batwing doors on to a sawdusted floor.

The saloon was his kind of place, bright and filled with glitter. The patrons – singles, pairs and small groups – had only bad words for the Yankees. 'Wouldn't give 'em the sweepings off'n the cotton-store floor,' he overheard one Anglo merchant say.

Jim bought beers, one after the other with dwindling money he could ill-afford, downing them till the harshness of thoughts, sights and sounds was reduced to a pleasant blur. Matt's shattering decision was still tragic, yet perhaps almost a mite comical, too.

The big room around him filled up, became smokier, noisier. Jim watched and wondered with nary a jot of concern where his next meal might be coming from. Someone played a jangly piano. A woman sang plaintively. Jim couldn't figure whether the words were Spanish or French, but he knew by instinct it was about love and loss. Exotic sadness. When his world had just about stopped turning, he looked up across the room . . . and saw Hook-Nose.

The man had to be the one who'd torched the Double H bunkhouse. Could two men have the same distinctive nose, the same bushy beard and unkempt, greasy hair?

Jim lurched to his feet instantly. 'Hey, you!' he cried, his own words ringing in his swimming head. 'I want you!'

He tried to make his way through the crowd. But he found his footing remarkably unsteady, and people somehow kept getting in his way. He stumbled into them, mumbled apologies, ploughed on, till one burly, teamster type affected to take umbrage. Afterward, Jim was to maintain the man deliberately blocked his passage toward Hook-Nose.

The latter had already turned tail and left the saloon in short order . . . which in itself was odd and tended to back Jim's suspicion he'd run across the murderous, fire-setting rustler who'd shot Walt Burridge, or accompanied the old-timer's killer.

'Don't shove me, feller!' the teamster said.

He swung a big-knuckled fist at Jim, who ducked but not fast enough to avoid being skittled as the blow slammed into his left shoulder.

'Fight! Fight!' yelled excited drinkers, thirsting for action. Not everyone here enjoyed melancholy melodies, it seemed.

Jim sprang gamely to his feet, the anaesthetizing beer fumes jarred from his body and head. But in his poor state, it didn't promise to be much of a fight.

He lammed one punch into the hard-muscled teamster's middle, but it was like hitting a rock. And the man again drew back his bunched right fist. Jim backed off till he was against a wall.

'Now hold hard, mister! There's no call—'

But the teamster wasn't interested in discussion; he meant to put him on the floor for keeps.

Jim went down fighting. He didn't cry out or even try to speak again. Other men might have done, but not Jim Hunter.

Less than two minutes later, he was lying senseless in the slops- and blood-spattered sawdust. The blood came from his own nose and a cut eye.

*

Consciousness returned painfully. Jim found it hard to open the swollen lids of his eyes. He had to struggle out of a darkened world shot through with bloody lightning.

He was lying on his back on a soft bed. Floral perfume was in the air and the sounds of the saloon were muffled and distant. Was he in a woman's bedroom?

He felt his face. It was a mass of throbbing bruises and sore, sticky splits. Curiosity and apprehension drove him to persist and force open his puffy eyelids.

He found he wasn't alone in the room, which he supposed to be above the saloon. A woman sat at a dressing-table mirror.

'I think you must be my Lady Luck,' he said. 'Why else am I in your room?' His head beat as he spoke as though it was being pounded with hammers.

The woman turned. 'Ah, so you are back with us, cowboy.'

He saw she was the bar-room singer. She had lustrous dark hair, full, painted red lips and a tall, shapely, very feminine body. Just at that moment, after fearing he might not see anything again, she was the most beautiful sight he'd set eyes on. Her skin was like cream on coffee; her eyes darkly sparkling. She wore a satiny red dress, trimmed with white lace. The décolletage was deep and Jim was aroused even in his groggy state.

The jewellery she wore was probably costume stuff for her performances – glittery rings on her slim fingers and gold hoops dangling from her ears.

'Why am I here?' he repeated.

'Because I had my brother Raoul and his fellows below carry you here, of course,' the young woman said in an attractive but cool and self-assured voice. Words and tone suggested she was that rarity among her sex – a woman who was a born leader and expected men do her bidding. 'Shame to see a strong and sassy man broken to no good purpose.'

'Who are you?' Jim asked, struggling to make sense of his rescue.

'My name is Lena-Marie Baptiste and my brother and I own this place.'

'Are you Mexican?'

'My! You are an enquiring man for one so busted up. No – my mother was Mexican, but my father was French and I was born and grew up in New Orleans.'

Jim tried to smile. 'Well, I'm much obliged to you, Miss Baptiste, but you must have had reason for picking up a beaten, tramp cowboy. I can't pay you.'

It was Lena-Marie's turn to smile. 'Not if what was in your pockets is all your wealth. But while you were out, you mumbled some ripe language about Yankees. I've got five hundred dollars urgently looking for a job that's made for a man who thinks that way. You ready to hear more?'

Jim tried harder to perk up. His interest was sparked both by the thought of $500 and the chance of getting to know its offerer a heap better.

'Sure I am! What kind of job is it?'

'Gun-running for the South. I work for the Confederacy and we have a shipment from Europe

23

stranded in a warehouse in Matamoros. I want it smuggled across the river and through the Northern Army lines to our hard-pressed troops. God knows those guns are needed! But it'll be dangerous and if you're caught, the Yankees will shoot or you or string you up from the gallows.'

Jim had never been short on courage or foolhardiness. Without Matt's influence to restrain him, he might long since have ridden off the straight and narrow trail. He didn't hesitate in accepting Lena-Marie's proposal.

'I'm your man, Miss Baptiste! I'm just itching to strike back at those bossy bluebellies.'

She laughed at his excitement. 'I like your enthusiasm. And you can call me Lena-Marie. . . . Now, what's your name, feller? I think we're going to have fun working together.'

They did. Jim soon led a band of like-minded compatriots and Mexicans who ran rings round the federal patrols with wagons that moved only by night. They safely shipped not one, but several loads of guns destined for the fighting in North Carolina. And when Jim wasn't cocking a snoot at Yankees, he and Lena-Marie found time to get to know one another – intimately.

With the beautiful Lena-Marie in his arms, all thought of Miss Alice Cornhill, of Trinity Creek, went out of Jim's mind.

'I've never loved anyone else quite like you,' he whispered, either telling a lie or forgetting, or a bit of both.

But all good things had to come to an end. One day, a soldier in ragged shirt and threadbare trousers that weren't just grey but faded grey, rode into Jim's camp on the Rio Grande. He swept off his crumpled kepi and mopped his sweating brow. He was in the lowest spirits.

'It's all done for,' he said. 'General Robert E. Lee's surrendered. He met Ulysses Grant at the McClean house in Appomattox, Virginia. They signed a paper. . . .'

It took a while for the seemingly gloomy news to sink in. Then, realization struck Jim Hunter. The South had lost, but the bloodshed and destruction were over. Peace had come.

His thoughts turned to his old friend Matt Harrison and their Double H ranch. With the war over, logically any differences they'd had were resolved.

Gladness welled up within him. It was time to go home; *to rebuild the Double H!*

The largest regret of his wartime adventures was that after that first day in Brownsville he'd never again sighted the murderer Hook-Nose.

Old Walt Burridge remained unavenged.

3

RETURN TO TRINITY CREEK

The Reconstruction had brought hardship to Texas. Livestock prices had tumbled, taking property values with them.

After nineteen months away, Jim Hunter rode the rutted, unrepaired road into Trinity Creek. All signs were of deferred maintenance and impending ruin. The fences and holding pens he saw on roadside properties were broken, sagging or plain gone rotten. A few head of cattle on a nearby pasture were spooked by the sight of a strange, lone rider and ran for the cover of a patch of scrub oak.

Poorly beasts, Jim told himself, a bunch of misbegotten longhorns maybe only lately dragged or hazed out of the mesquite by ex-soldiers returning from war.

It was a matter of considerable speculation to him

whether the Double H could be successfully revived in these prevailing conditions of extremity. Much would depend on re-establishing contact with Matt Harrison, to which purpose he was headed for the Trinity Creek township. The two H's had had accounts there with storekeepers, the local country lawyer, the doctor and other businesses, plus friends like pretty Miss Alice Cornhill and her mother, Mrs Alberta Cornhill.

Someone, surely, would have heard from Matt or know of his whereabouts.

Soberly, Jim was reminded that many of the sons of Texas would not be returning home. Fully a fourth of able-bodied men had been lost in the war. Others were maimed and would never work again. Yet others had no stomach for Yankee rule and had fled to more promising territories. Carpetbaggers from the North had moved in, quickly establishing themselves in commerce and government. They often employed strongarmed and underhand methods to secure their ends.

Maybe Matt would be one of those who could not or would not come back to his old stamping grounds. But at least he had picked the right side in the conflict, Jim thought ruefully.

Trinity Creek was like its surroundings – run-down. Some of its stores were boarded up and most could do with cleaning and a lick of paint. He noticed a bunch of four men in Union uniform, apparently idling on the main street. They looked shiftless riff-raff rather than decent troopers. In Jim's opinion, the best of the Yankee fighters had returned home to pick up their civilian lives. These were died-in-the-wool drifters – hoboes by calling – with no home, no trade, no honour.

Conscious of his grey army coat, he steered clear of them and headed for McAuley's Mercantile Store. It was still the biggest emporium in town and looked to have prospered, relatively. Well, of course it had . . . Alexander McAuley, always a big noise in town affairs, had never made any bones about his Union sympathies. The new times would favour him.

At the last moment, Jim changed his mind about going to the pompous, autocratic merchant and turned his feet toward the man's handsome home in the town's best residential section a few blocks away.

Here, he knew he'd find Alice Cornhill. Because the community had no formal school, she provided basic teaching in a spacious back room for widower McAuley's six children. McAuley was also the Cornhills' landlord and in consideration for Alice's efforts he reduced a ridiculously high rent for a mean and shabby cottage to ten dollars month.

Jim's spirits lifted at the thought of seeing Alice again. He also felt a twinge of guilty conscience. In the heady exhilaration of his relationship with Lena-Marie Baptiste in Brownsville, he'd almost allowed Alice to be wiped from his mind. Foolish. . . .

Lena-Marie had been an adventuress, just as he had been an adventurer. Circumstances had thrown them together. Their liaison, though physically fulfilling and satisfying their needs at the time wholly, had had no deeper significance than any other plea-suring of body and senses.

Alice was altogether something else. Gracious, pure and sweet. . . .

The only characteristic he could think of that Alice and Lena-Marie had in common was that both gave the lie to the uncharitable claim that girls who were beautiful tended to be very little else.

Looking forward to seeing again Alice's pretty form, her clear skin, blue eyes and golden hair, Jim hurried his steps to the schoolroom's porch.

He met with disappointment. When the door was opened in response to his knock, it was not by Alice but by a hard-faced, young woman stranger.

'Yes?'

'Oh! I was looking for Miss Cornhill.'

'Gone. Passed up her chance, didn't she?'

'What do you mean?'

The woman lifted her shoulders. With a scornful twist of her mouth, she said off-handedly, impertinently, 'Thought she was too good for McAuley and the sly side of the job, I guess. Ought to have growed up. Learned a few things about life. Now I'm the schoolma'am, ain't I?'

Most of this sounded like riddles to Jim. But he couldn't imagine anyone less like a schoolmistress than this person. A mistress, more like. Her face was painted and powdered and her eyes full of a knowing that didn't come from books. She reeked of cheap perfume and reminded Jim of an essentially vapid but unscrupulous whore.

He asked, 'Are the Cornhills still in Trinity Creek, at Mr McAuley's cottage?'

'No.'

'Do you know where they've gone?'

The woman hesitated momentarily. 'No.'

Jim thought she lied, but he tried a new approach. 'I'm really looking for a Matt Harrison who had a spread in these parts.'

He still won no respect, not even civility.

'Better go there then, hadn't you?' his unhelpful informant said.

'I'm fixing to do that.'

'Can't keep you from it nohow, I'm sure.'

He felt derision in the way she looked at him and saw a fresh sneer of something akin to triumph on her ugly lips. He decided he was wasting his time.

'Thank you, missy,' he said, equally sarcastically. 'And good day.'

She slammed the door as he turned and left.

Jim headed out of town and gave his horse its head. The sun was bright in a clear and cloudless sky and man's neglect of his enterprises seemed of lesser importance in open country.

But the spectacle that gladdened his heart most, coming in sight of the Double H ranch, was a strong-armed, lone man repairing a pole corral fence.

'By all the saints – Matt Harrison!' Jim breathed aloud. 'He's gotten here ahead of me. Ain't that grand?'

He felt sure the woman at McAuley's must have known. She'd been holding out on him. He couldn't see why she should have been so difficult and smug. She must have known he'd find out his friend had arrived before him.

Men like Matt were salt of the earth, the kind of men who could build the West: solid, hardworking, with many practical skills like animal husbandry – or fence building. He was a methodical man, sandy-haired with freckles and a redly weathered face. There was a certain reassurance in his familiar, stocky frame.

Jim called out his name and he turned and dropped his hammer.

'Jim!' he cried. 'Jim Hunter, by all that's wonderful. We'd about given you up for dead! God be praised you ain't.'

Jim rode up and swung down and they flung their arms around each other.

'So you're out of the Union Army, Matt.'

'Yes. I've seen too much dying. They were signing on boys to fight Injuns when I drew my pay, but fighting and killing is no profession for me, Jim. Like Lincoln said, it's time to bind up the nation's wounds, and that's what I'm doing here, back home. I'm real glad you've made it back safely, too. Now the place can properly become the old Double H again.'

Jim was enthusiastic. He'd seen that elsewhere in Texas violence and bitterness were rampant between those who'd supported the Confederacy and those who'd been Union sympathizers and were now enjoying their day in the sun. But none of that would come between himself and Matt making a new success of the Double H. Hadn't Matt voiced an optimism that the ranch could be rehabilitated? As peace established itself, the lives of fair-minded people such as themselves could only improve.

'I'll be right beside you, just like before. No one can pay much for beef in these parts, but up North the price is recovering, they say. We could round up a herd, fatten it and drive it to a railhead, I reckon.'

Matt chuckled. 'Whoa! You're right. More hands will make lighter work, but we have a heap to catch up on before that. Things were let go to hell, as you can see.'

What Jim saw mostly was that the bunkhouse and barn were still nothing but charred sticks on blackened dirt, but all the sprawling ranch house's doors and windows had been unboarded and showed signs of freshness and life. Curtains flapped at the windows. Even before, they'd never had curtains and they lent a homely touch. Incredibly, it looked, too, as though Matt had started a small vegetable and flower garden on the south side of the house.

'You've already been busy, Matt,' Jim said.

Matt looked wary and a little sheepish. 'I have, but let's go to the house. There's much to tell you.'

'Sure. I can give you a hand to finish up with the fence later. Guess I've got a lot of stories to tell myself.'

They trudged toward the house, Jim leading his horse.

It occurred to Jim he was bringing nothing to the revived venture except his labour.

'Are there debts?' he asked guiltily. 'Like, I heard some ranches are being confiscated by the courts to pay back taxes. The Yankee judges take a hard line on Texans, it seems.'

Matt seemed almost relieved to address the topic.

'I used up most of my army pay to clear what we owed, Jim. So there's nothing to worry about on that count.'

Then, before more could be said, there was a rush of movement behind the curtain-framed windows of the ranch house lying ahead of them and a young woman rushed out on to its veranda, wearing an apron. She wiped her hands on it and seemed to jump like an excited child. She waved at them happily.

'Why, it's my Alice!' Jim exclaimed in astonishment. He quickly corrected his presumption. 'Miss Alice Cornhill.'

Matt coughed, but the hand he raised to his mouth was to cover his plunge into mumbling embarrassment.

'Actually, Mrs Matthew Harrison now. . . .'

4

ORDEAL OF
THE HEART

Both Matt and Alice had reacted instantaneously and warmly to his return to the Double H. Matt had embraced him; Alice had jumped with joy. But the shared pleasure of their reunion was swiftly snuffed out as the implications of the situation dawned.

Mrs Harrison. . . Alice had become Matt's wife!

Jim felt the blood drain from his face and his devastation was clearly apparent to Alice, who lowered her eyes and whose voice trembled.

'Why, Jim, it's lovely to see you again. I didn't think we ever would.'

The last time they'd been together, all three had accepted that Alice Cornhill was Jim's sweetheart; that it was only a matter of time before he popped the question which Matt apparently had.

Jim cursed. 'The war! The damned war! It's changed everything!'

He should have known something was wrong with the setup at the ranch when he'd seen the new flower and vegetable garden outside the kitchen door; the curtains at the windows.

Alice's mother, the widow Mrs Alberta Cornhill, had always taken in sewing in Trinity Creek to provide herself and her daughter with an income of a basic sort. Jim made a gallant attempt to lift the chill that had descended on them in the comfortable but simply furnished front parlour.

'I can see your ma's been busy, too. The curtains are very pretty.'

Alice looked at him with tears welling in her eyes.

'I made them myself. Mama died six months past.'

'Oh God,' Jim groaned. 'I'm sorry. I didn't know.'

'How could you?' Alice sat down on a sofa. 'The first hint she was poorly came very sudden. One night about eleven o'clock, I heard her breathing very hard—'

'Alice!' Matt said. 'You mustn't upset yourself.'

'I won't, Matt dear, but I do believe it's fair we should tell Jim everything.'

Matt sighed and she went on.

'I got up from my bed and called to Mama, because the sound was so strange. She gave no answer, so I went to her, to find her wide awake but speechless. I tried to raise her but she'd no more power in her limbs than a baby and fell back on the bed. I ran for Doc Brandon.'

Jim admired Alice anew for the composure she'd

35

summoned to tell her story, but he felt constrained to protest.

'Alice, you don't have to put yourself through this for me.'

'But I want to, Jim. And I can see it is owed – all of it.'

'Very well,' he said gruffly. 'As you choose. I'll not interrupt again.'

'The doctor was out of town, delivering a baby,' Alice went on. 'When he eventually came, he bled Mama and said she'd had a stroke. She was very ill and had lost her speech and the use of the left side of her body. Well, she took a heavy cold, then a cough and fever. It was a merciful release when my mother breathed her last twelve days later. I was kneeling at her bedside, my prayer book in one hand and her hand in my other, when she passed away. I think I was exhausted from watching over her, but my trials were only just beginning.'

Matt broke in this time.

'It was that animal Alexander McAuley! He'd been paying unwarranted attentions to Alice for months. You know his much-suffering wife was long dead and unmourned from the day she was buried. With Mrs Cornhill departed, the swine allowed his lusts for Alice into the open. He demanded her body, with or without matrimony, as well as free tuition for his snivelling brood.'

'Matt!' Alice objected. 'Let me tell it my way, without dwelling on the unseemliness.'

'Forgive me. I forget my manners when I think of McAuley.'

36

'Mr McAuley had always been a – *difficult* land-lord,' she explained to Jim. 'Mama said oftentimes I should marry a good man to put an end to his nonsense. When she died, and Mr McAuley redoubled his pestering, it was most fortunate for me that Matt should offer his hand in marriage, and a safe home.'

Jim was beginning to form the picture. Matt – steady, reliable Matt – had chosen the right side in the war and was the more accessible as a member of a regular army. Alice, though still not twenty, was a progressive thinker and sympathetic to causes like women's emancipation. She loved Texas and had once extolled to Jim its atmosphere of democracy, equality and opportunity. She had strongly opposed slavery, however.

Sensing an injustice to himself, he said, 'I always planned to come back, Alice, and I never endorsed slavery.'

'Oh, Jim!' Alice said. 'Do I hear blame in your voice? Matt and I will always love you, whatever your beliefs. But your movements were shrouded in mystery and uncertainty. We heard you were riding with guerrilla bands – irregulars – who assisted the pro-slavery faction.'

'I brought guns from Matamoros to the Texas Confederate Army.'

'Yes! Fearsome, dangerous work, with death apt to lurk behind every other bush, Jim. Such service was mad folly, but it wasn't the reason I didn't wait for you. Matt is a good, fine man. My mother always felt it better I should encourage him rather than yourself. Small wonder when she was taken from me that I should turn to him! I was left alone – flung by cruel circumstance at the mercy of Mr McAuley who insisted I should attend his bedroom as well as his children's schoolroom. When I refused, he threw me out on the street and replaced me with another.'

'An insult for a replacement!' Jim railed.

'Ah, so you've met Miss Ruby Smith?'

'I did. She'd not be my choice to teach school. A baggage no better than she should be, for sure!'

'Or a woman, if I may say so, of lapsed virtue and therefore much better suited for all Mr McAuley had in mind.'

'In short, she's a trollop, Alice.'

'Which I am not. Matt is the good knight who saved me from her fate.'

Matt sat on the arm of the sofa and put his arm round her shoulders.

'I made our ranch Alice's sanctuary, Jim.'

Alice lifted her firm chin. 'In my darkest hour, Matt brought me love and protection in a world too full of its own tribulations to care what happened to one ordinary girl. Meanwhile, Jim Hunter was a will o' the wisp I might never see again. Indeed, the Confederate die-hards are fighting still. They refuse to surrender. We read in a paper just yesterday of a skirmish at a ranch outside of Brownsville. Now do you understand?'

Jim said he did, but he didn't really know if it was the truth.

War had tested his daring and he'd survived; had his small triumphs on the back of wild decisions that had unnerved his friends and his comrades. The new question was, would peace leave him as unscathed?

The days slipped by into weeks. Trying to restore the Double H to its former glory was hard work for the two men. They had no money to hire hands, though they had hopes of rounding up a herd from strays and mavericks. The effort on this front and on the ranch buildings continued from daybreak to sundown six days a week. Alice insisted they should rest some on Sundays.

They roped calves, dragged them to fires along with their mothers, gave them identical, Double H brands on their hips and earmarked them. The nicks would help Jim and Matt readily recognize the critters later when the hair had grown back to obscure the branding mark and they wanted to assemble a selection for the trail north.

Matt was optimistic. 'Now there's the two of us, I think the Double H can make it. We did it before, remember? We can sell a few head locally, even though prices are poor, and put together a crew for the drive.'

It was a tiring business, needing hourly changes of horses. The calves and cows bawled and struggled. The air was filled with the stench of burning hair. The day's work left the men hot, sweaty and exhausted.

And at nights, Jim also found himself stewing. The sleep and rest he needed was denied him as he tossed and turned, his thoughts and emotions in turmoil.

He learned that wounds could be received of a

kind no soldier encountered on a battlefield. Without a barn or bunkhouse to which he might escape, he was obliged to sleep under the same roof as his married friends.

The house was sprawling and its exterior walls solid, but it was not so well built that, in the quiet and the darkness, sounds didn't travel within from one end to the other, through doors and partition walls. Jim put his head under his blankets to muffle them, but still he would hear the gasps, moans and sighs of unbridled passion. He tortured himself, visualizing Matt's stubby fingers, with sandy hair sprouting from the backs of the lower joints, exploring all the secret parts of Alice's adorable body. Occasionally, her unmistakable love-cries were multiple and of mounting intensity.

The following day, he would find it hard to let his eyes meet either hers or Matt's. If anything, his physical longing for Alice was doubled by the constant reminders she was no longer a virgin and was initiated into the ways of pleasing a man. Possibly the couple didn't realize how noise travelled through the house, or were oblivious to anyone or anything but themselves when they were carried away by such matters.

Jim knew Alice still liked him and wondered at times if, when Matt was away in town or off on some solo chore in an outlying pasture, she would be willing to ease his torment and indulge at least her curiosity about him. He was convinced it hadn't diminished in the many months he'd been away. Of all the many things that had changed, their attraction to each other had not. Nothing could restore

Alice's former innocence – it was ruined and done – yet the loss could also be a gain of compensatory experience. Also, being a married woman would surely add convenience in case of unplanned consequences. . . .

These were the alluring directions in which Jim's fevered thoughts ran.

'We could do it discreetly, delicately,' he wanted to suggest, but at heart he knew Alice was a God-fearing woman and would never break her marriage vows, however much she might be tempted. The promising days when they'd been sweethearts, able to contemplate some future, mysterious bliss, had gone for ever. Alice's bereavement, her subsequent hardship – about which she'd say little – and her marriage had given her new strength of character that made her no less desirable.

Laden with frustration and despair, Jim was finally forced to reconsider his presence on the Double H.

Shirts off, he and Matt were washing off the worst of the day's dirt before entering the house after another day's hard labour.

'The hell with it, Matt,' he announced dismally. 'This is a decision I never wanted to make, but I have to or I'll go mad, do something reckless, or considerable worse. . . .'

Matt sloshed the dirty water from a tin washbasin across the dusty yard and reached for a towel. 'What on earth are you blathering about, Jim?'

'I'm leaving. If I stay on at the Double H, someone's going to get hurt real bad. You or me or . . . *Alice.*'

'I don't understand, Jim. We both want you here. The Double H needs you. This is crazy talk.'

'No, it ain't, goddamnit! Living in the same place as you with Alice as your wife is more than flesh and blood can stand.'

Matt was bewildered and stared at Jim like he'd been hit hard and stunned.

'Don't talk that way. It's different from before, I'll allow, but time will make it right.'

'No, it won't. Time is only making it worse. You might be great with animals, Matt, but you don't understand people. I love Alice – always did – wanted her desperately since she was scarce more than a kid. One thing the war hasn't changed is that I still do. Now she can't be a wife to me, it's wrong.'

Matt looked stricken, but a certain sympathy also dawned in the depths of his blue eyes. 'Our marriage was a shock to you, Jim. You'll heal. . . .'

The suggestion did no good. Jim held to his harshness.

'I know what I need to do, and it's get clear out of here. Let's go tell Alice I'm quitting directly, but not a real word of why, please.'

In the greyness of early morning after Jim had announced he was leaving and while the air still had its pre-dawn chill, Alice watched as Jim carefully saddled the big chestnut gelding on which he'd arrived, got his bags and tied them on with his roll of blankets and slicker.

Alice Harrison, née Cornhill, was nobody's fool. She knew Jim Hunter had found it impossible to get over her being Matt's woman. The pair of them had not spoken of it to her. Brave, handsome, worthy and intelligent men though they both were, they were silly enough to suppose she was unaware of the situation.

She went out to the men with a small sack of supplies – beans, flour, bacon, dried fruit and coffee.

'For the trail,' she said simply.

Jim thanked her and tied the sack on, too, behind the saddle.

Matt said, 'You don't have to do this, Jim. We're still your friends.'

'I know you are. Howsoever, I have to go.'

It's why I have to go, is what Alice imagined he wanted to say.

'But where to? What will you do?'

Jim's reply to Matt's enquiry was casually voiced, but Alice thought he was straining for the tone.

'Thought maybe I'd head for the coast. I've a hankering to see the ocean again. My Brownsville friends were fixing to set up in some fishing village. Maybe I'll rejoin them.'

Alice felt a pang of disquiet. The people Jim had run with during the war had been of dubious character in her opinion – adventurers and fortune hunters more concerned with their own ambitions than causes. She suspected the rebellion of the Confederacy had been a train for them to jump, promising to carry its riders to excitement and riches.

Whatever Jim's erstwhile friends were up to now, she had a premonition it would be sure to end in no good. Oh, Jim. . . she cried, but dared to utter the cry only inwardly.

'Well, don't forget us when you tire of the sea, will you?' she said with forced lightness. 'Come visit us sometime.'

Jim laughed artificially. 'I'll bring you a canteenful of the briny.'

Then, after an exchange of grunted 'see yous', Jim mounted up and rode out, heading into an eastern sky touched with rose.

Alice noted her husband's flushed face and the way he shuffled his feet in the dirt of the yard. He plainly felt awkward, but he was sorry for himself, too.

'On paper, we're still fifty-fifty with Jim,' he told her with a growling despair. 'But how can I make a go of the Double H without him?'

Her short married life with Matt had seemed bright, happy, clean and promising, until his prodigal partner and her one-time beau had reappeared.

'Maybe his friends won't be there on the Gulf. Maybe he'll come back,' she said with faint hope.

'No. The war has changed Jim – made him bitter. He's gotten a poor attitude.'

Bitter? Alice didn't think so. At bottom, Jim was happy-go-lucky; he shunned the drear and disappointing. He hated restriction and had always shown an inclination to taste and enjoy the forbidden. If anyone had acquired a poor attitude, it was Matt. He expected too much of Jim, who had shown a certain bravery by riding out.

She could see full well why Jim was quitting the

pain of shared life with his friends on the Double H; to stay and possibly succumb to temptation would have been treachery.

And she understood all of this so well because her own heart ached.

The sun was rising but Alice felt like it was going down on her world.

5

HOOK-NOSE?

Palmito was nothing much – a one-time wholly Mexican place of adobe and clapboard someplace north of the Rio Grande on the Gulf Coast, originally founded in the mid 1700s when General José de Escandon had been appointed by Spain to colonize Tamaulipas.

After three gruelling days of crossing sandy desert terrain, Jim Hunter rode into an isolated and what looked an unproductive seaside settlement. A cluster of dilapidated fishing shacks denoted a port area where a rock and lumber jetty jutted punily into the vastness of a blue bay, bordered way out by the white-rimmed shore of a reef.

The town behind had narrow alleys between structures with windowless walls and closed doors. Trash had been left to rot and stink in the blistering sun and salt air back of the buildings on its main street.

Unfavourably impressed, Jim turned his horse into

a livery barn in what looked like the newest section of town. He'd ridden far and Palmito was the only civilization in miles, so for the moment he had no option.

The hostler was a wrinkled, dried-up oldster in a dirty grey army coat with one sleeve empty and pinned up. He didn't pause in chewing his tobacco, but looked Jim up and down as though challenging him to speak the first words.

'Take care of my bronc, mister?' Jim asked. At least the familiar smells of hay and manure were strong and welcoming.

The one-armed man ejected a stream of brown from between his stained whiskers. It landed with a splat, forming a dark, phlegmy glob on the dust just inches away from the front hoofs of Jim's chestnut.

'Mebbe, cowboy. It's a buck a day – in advance. Yuh got real money?'

Jim nodded. 'I got some.'

'Have to ask, yuh unnerstan. Confederacy paper ain't worth shit no more. 'Course, we had nothin' else when we was cut off durin' the Union Navy's blockade. Now it's all gold an' silver eagles.'

Jim looked up the straw-littered aisle and out through the barn's big double doors. 'Not much sign of it at work.'

The oldster chortled. 'The town ain't all a dump no more, cowboy. Five merchants, a banker an' a few others set up here since the war was over.'

Jim got down from the saddle. He wondered aloud what sustained this investment. 'Seems kind of grand for an out-of-the-way, two-bit burg.'

'Yuh askin' questions, feller?' the chewing hostler said. And his eyes narrowed as Jim unsaddled his horse.

'No. Only where I might find my friends, name of Baptiste. Miss Lena-Marie and Raoul.'

He threw the saddle over a rack. The hostler, leading the horse into a stall, sized him up in a fresh light.

He said shrewdly, 'Uh-huh. If'n it's fer a fact yuh're an amigo, I guess the Baptistes'll be plumb satisfied to answer your questions their ownselves. Yuh'll find 'em at their Gulf Trader Saloon. Sure 'nuff yuh won't miss it.'

Jim discovered that was so. The saloon, a two-storey frame building, was one of the places in town that hadn't gone to seed. The exterior was freshly painted, fancy lace curtains backed panes of clean glass, the sign that proclaimed its name was no crude scrawl but a legend in ornate lettering. Inside, a piano played tunefully. Everything suggested the interior would be citified and fancy, with expensive mirrors, gilt-framed pictures by prominent artists, solid, hand-carved furniture and chandeliers.

Striding up to the swing doors, Jim was taken by surprise when they were flung almost into his face.

The man who emerged was not so much in a hurry as arrogant. He had the bearing of a fellow for whom others habitually made way.

'Easy, mister,' Jim said as the man about shouldered him off the saloon's front veranda. 'I don't like being shoved around.'

The man snarled. 'And I don't like your talk,

48

tramp!' With that he hit Jim across the mouth with the back of his hand.

Jim was startled because it happened so quickly, but what gave him cause for greater astonishment was dawning recognition. At first, he didn't know if he could believe his eyes, but his assailant was the image of Hook-Nose – the killer he'd been longing to run across since that one fateful night shortly before he and Matt had gone to Brownsville and war.

Hook-Nose's beard had been shaggy, his hair straggly. This man's beard was more of a fringe running from sideburn to sideburn and his hair was cut short. But his nose was decidedly hooked. Surely they had to be one and the same.

Jim swallowed his disbelief and his outrage at being struck.

'I know you, mister!' he spat. 'You're an arsonist, a killer and a rustler!'

Hook-Nose looked at him blankly. 'What the hell is this? Git outa my way!'

'You killed Walt Burridge, burned me out of the Double H in the Trinity Creek country. Now's the showdown!'

'I don't know what yuh're rantin' about, yuh goddamn loon. Back off!'

But a flicker of something – recognition, memory? – showed in the protester's cold, snake eyes.

What Jim had to do was clear in his mind. Seeing this man revived the horror of Old Walt's murder and the fury that had never really left him. Though not a violent man by choosing, he would kill inoffensive Walt's vile and contemptible killer calmly and dispassionately. Do it and still live with his conscience.

'I saw you once, soon after in Brownsville, but this time you can't dodge me and you're going to die. When I count three, go for your gun! One . . . two . . . three—'

Hook-Nose realized Jim wasn't to be deterred. 'All right, Mr Smartass, yuh asked for it!'

As Jim's right hand dipped to the butt of the six-shooter at his hip, he drew himself. And he was greased lightning. Both men's sideguns left their holsters simultaneously. Each gun pointed at the other at a range of scant feet.

Neither fired. Jim knew – and knew Hook-Nose knew – that the moment either pulled trigger, so would the other. Death would be a shared lot.

Hook-Nose, though he had to have been surprised by Jim's gunspeed, sneered at the standoff. Jim said icily, 'I'm still going to kill you. Holster your gun and we'll try again. This time, you count.'

But what Jim overlooked was that Hook-Nose had friends in the saloon. They'd been witnessing the events unfolding just outside with growing fascination. The moment the pair's weapons were back in their holsters – Hook-Nose still complacent – they boiled out through the doors, confident they weren't going to run directly into blazing guns.

'Fix the stupid son of a bitch, boys!' Hook-Nose rapped.

The order was superfluous. Jim was bowled off his feet by the bunch. One of the three who struck him bodily fell with him. Twisting as he hit the boards with a thump, Jim snatched out his gun again. He brought its iron down on the head of the man grappling him. The man slumped and released his grip.

But it was impossible for Jim to beat the uneven odds and rise.

The gun was kicked from his fist and went clattering into the shadows. More punishing kicks rolled him off the veranda, down the wooden steps and on to the hard and dusty roadway.

The gang kept after him, kicking and punching each time he tried to get up. Only by will power did he fight to his knees, then to his feet. His arms moved like pistons, but like his legs they were numbed by the blows he'd collected. His ribs and belly were bruised from the gang's kicks and breathing was difficult, the air whistling painfully in his throat.

Jim figured he ought to try to run, but perhaps they wouldn't let him go now, and quitting a fight – even an unfair one – went against his nature. Damn them, before he went down he'd give an account of himself Hook-Nose's bully-boys would remember. They'd have to break his bones before they broke his spirit.

He swung a bunch of grazed knuckles at a crooked grin on a lean face. The blur of his own motion ended in a paralysing jolt as he connected with the long chin. Satisfyingly, something exploded with a crack that sounded like dynamite in his ringing ears.

The lanky brawler slumped to the ground unconscious. For a moment, Jim thought he'd broken clear, but the rest of his attackers advanced in a semicircle, closing in on him. One of them lunged, hitting Jim with a looping right and bringing up a knee to his groin in a vicious follow-up. Fortunately, Jim was able to turn and absorb most of the kneeing with his thigh. He slammed the man savagely in the throat. The dirty fighter whirled away, gasping and choking.

Jim's own breath came in harsh, wheezing grunts.

'Bastards! This ain't a fair fight.'

Instinctively, he knew it was hopeless. Put one down, even two, and others would take their place. He was the stranger here and the sheer force of numbers would eventually take its toll. The battle could end only one way – he would be beaten to a pulp. Already his senses were reeling, fading to brief blackness, then clearing before repeating the cycle. He felt he'd been pounded like meat into a total mass of sapping bruises and aches that went bone-deep. In truth, he was in excruciating pain.

Surrounded on all sides, he was pummelled by a new flurry of blows. He felt skin and flesh split at brow, cheek and mouth. The blood ran freely.

Suddenly, out of the corner of his eye, he caught new movement. A figure had emerged on to the upstairs balcony over the saloon doors. A voice yelled an order in words he couldn't make out. The order was followed by a roar that smashed through the air over his head like a deafening thunderclap. A pattering in the dust beyond the fighting men was marked more by small upflingings of dust than its sound, which was lost in the echoes of the greater crash.

The fighting stopped instantly.

The voice said with a hard edge, 'Break it up, fellers, or I'll empty the second barrel right in the middle of you, damnit! And you know what a charge of buck from a ten-gauge does to targets close as yourselves.'

Jim looked up. He knew the voice; he recognized the man. It was Raoul Baptiste.

Baptiste meant business. When Jim's attackers backed off, he broke the smoking scattergun. He punched in a live shell from a pocket to replace the one he'd expended. He closed the shotgun with a snap and thumbed back the right hammer.

He looked smart as well as commanding. Clean-shaven save for a dark, narrow line of moustache above his thin upper lip, he was dressed in the style of a Mexican grandee with a ruffed white silk shirt, tightly cut black pants and a red sash wound around his waist. A man of substance in an unexpected setting. From the first glance, Jim understood plainly Raoul Baptiste had a measure of authority beside the gun. He surely cut a dash in this hick town.

Around Jim, sullen and hesitant riff-raff edged away nervously. Standing back, Hook-Nose looked smug. It was all becoming a blur. Jim raised the back of a hand to his brow to wipe away the blood trickling into his eyes.

But it wasn't that alone obscuring his vision. His hearing, too, was failing and it had nothing to do with the dramatic reverberations of the shotgun.

The blackness and the roaring intensified and finally, though the punishing fight was over, he felt himself falling, falling. . . .

He came round lying on a bed in a room filled with a woman's floral perfume. He frowned without opening his eyes to the brightness that showed redly through the lids. Somehow, time must have slipped. He felt, with a sense of unreality, he was replaying a scene from his past life.

'Brownsville. . . ?' he murmured aloud. 'No, I ain't there. Can't be there.'

'The French call it *déjà vu*,' a familiar voice said with a lilt.

Lena-Marie Baptiste. Just like when he'd first met her after being thrashed by the burly teamster in Brownsville. And she, too, was aware of the irony.

'Jim, *querido mio*! You have a propensity for arriving places and getting into scrapes.'

'No, I ain't,' Jim mumbled through thick lips. 'It was the same damn thing again. I saw *him* – the man who murdered Walt Burridge and I've sworn to send to hell!'

'Peace, Jim, peace.'

He forced his eyes open. Lena-Marie was bent over him. A hint of amusement was mingled with the concern on her beautiful face.

'I'm in Palmito, aren't I? Did Raoul have me brought in here? How long have I been out?'

'Questions! Questions! Me, I'm only glad to see you again. Dare I hope you've tired of your smelly cattle spread and come to join us. . .?' She raised slender fingers to her full red lips. 'Oh! Now you have me doing it!'

Jim swallowed. He was aroused. In spite of his pains, the sight of her sent his pulses racing as they always had. Physically, nothing could appeal to him more than to make love with her again, even though he knew she also dispensed her favours elsewhere with judgement and guile. Lena-Marie was a woman of the world, a mistress of situations as well as men, and he'd seen during the war that her doings could be figured to serve practical ends.

Nature had equipped her magnificently for her chosen role. She reminded him of a mountain lioness, lithe, supple and with a big cat's smooth, silent grace. Her exotic attractiveness exuded subtle challenge.

'Right now I could use a drink,' he said, playing for time.

He hadn't the wits yet to enter into her games, much as he wanted to find out what went on in this unlovely town to attract her like. In peacetime, what new rackets were afoot? What new webs of deception was she weaving?

'But of course,' she said. 'And we must celebrate your return to our fold with better than water.'

She left the room and it felt empty, drained of its colour without her vitality but retaining her aura. He knew she'd had him brought to a room that was one of her own.

She returned quickly with a tray carrying glasses and a bottle of genuine French brandy.

'Only the best for you, *muy caballero.*'

She poured generous measures. She smiled invitingly into his eyes as she handed him one of the full glasses. Without any doubt, her look said, she would be his for the taking soon as he was fit and ready.

She lifted her glass and lightly touched it to his. 'To our reunion,' she whispered throatily. 'Let us drain our glasses to the coming good times!'

'Yeah,' he agreed thickly. But in his mind he added the rider that before he rehitched his wagon to the Baptistes, he would need to know first what she and Raoul had turned their hands to in this dead-end place.

What was the source of their latest opulence?

Where did the man he was certain was Hook-Nose and his roughneck followers fit in?

Were killers part of the Baptistes' setup?

6

SOUTH OF
THE LAW

A tense, strained atmosphere hung in the small, white-walled office back of the Gulf Trader.

'You are being very cautious,' Lena-Marie said softly. 'You should trust me, Jim. Or are you afraid?'

Maybe he should trust her. For he'd had four free nights of the Baptistes' hospitality. The last two, he'd shared Lena-Marie's bed. It had been an exciting, very satisfying experience, renewing their old intimacy. But he'd not taken total leave of his overheated senses.

He was still mindful Lena-Marie was an alluring, walking man-trap. During the war, many red-blooded Union officers had learned this – but invariably only when it was too late to retract snippets of vital information. They'd let them slip to their side's cost in pillow talk between the satin sheets of a bed where she daringly relieved men of secrets in addition to the frustrations stored up by front-line service.

'I think we have a lot to talk about,' he prevaricated. It was as well the conversation was not taking place someplace else; that they were seated either side of a handsome, craftsman-made oak desk. It made it easier to stay level-headed.

Her brother Raoul's presence also made it clear this was strictly business. The shade was pulled down at the window and he propped himself up against the wall alongside it, dragging on a long black cigarette. One of its kin, which came from a slim, gold case, smouldered in an ashtray on the desk, close to his sister's elegant, jewelled-ringed hand.

'But we've already talked,' Lena-Marie said in a bantering tone. 'We want you to work with us again, to share our good fortune in the shipping business here, from the import and export of merchandise across the Mexican border.'

Jim said boldly, 'Besides running the saloon and the town's only bordello, you have a new twist on smuggling in peacetime, you mean. You ignore the federal laws.'

'Like we ever did,' Raoul put in with less patience than his sister. 'We do great good in Palmito. The populace was on its knees when we came. The wartime blockade, a severe drought in 1863 and a frigid winter in 1864 had brought almost total economic collapse and famine. Even before the hostilities, the town endured attacks and robberies by gangs and cattle rustlers. Citizens begged for government intervention at national and regional level, but little help came.'

Lena-Marie briefly drew on her cigarette; tapped ash from it delicately.

'What Raoul says is true,' she said. 'Texans have long known the area south of the Nueces River, including Palmito, as the "dead line of sheriffs". There is no law in place for us to break. We are benefactors, but must provide ourselves and the community with private protection. Which means hiring former irregulars like you.'

Jim said, 'Also, the hook-nosed man you call Woodson Waldrop. I've seen too much of Reconstruction law to have any respect for it, but Waldrop must be brought to justice. He was a cattle rustler and the member of a gang such as Raoul describes. The very type in point of fact!'

'I think you might be mistaken, Jim . . .' Lena-Marie said airily. She leaned back in the broad swivel chair behind the desk with the easy laziness of a stretching wildcat. Her full breasts thrust distractingly at the thin fabric of her blouse. Jim thought of cupping them again in his hands, uncovered and stimulatingly alive.

'Woody and his gang worked for us during the war,' she went on. 'They were a Confederate militia company. Like you, they participated in the gun-running operation from Mexico.'

Jim growled. 'I figure he must've found time to do some hell-raising of his own; for burning Matt and me out of the Double H . . . killing our hand, a harmless old-timer.'

She shrugged. 'I can say no more than I know.

Listen, Jim, the war is over. You know that – you know all things have changed. Your attempted shootout with Woody was ridiculous. You have no proof of his identity as the man who wronged you. Why not let it rest?'

Jim wavered under the warm gaze of her dark-lashed eyes. The knot of desire tightened in him. Gruffly, he acknowledged her doubts.

'All right. Maybe I was a touch hasty. I'll give you this – I agree to hold my peace till I can check it out.'

Lena-Marie and Raoul's offer of work, a home and a thrillingly warmed bed was temptation he couldn't resist.

'So you are with us, Jim?'

'Sure, I'm with you.'

For a backwater coastal town, Jim found Palmito wasn't doing too badly. The Baptistes had raised the money to dredge its ship channel several feet, which in turn was attracting other businessmen and investment. But the continuing lack of a real, deep-water port still forced ships to anchor offshore and load all cargo into smaller vessels. This limited development of trade.

The town's banker, a newcomer from the North sometimes dubbed a carpetbagger, spoke boldly of plans for more dredging and for introducing a bill in the state legislature to incorporate a Palmito and Rio Grande Railroad which would link the town and Rio Grande City to San Antonio and Brownsville. He was promoting a Palmito City Company to attract more investment.

'Palmito will emerge as a vital exporter of South Texas cattle and sheep,' he promised, polishing his gold-rimmed spectacles. 'Within a decade, there'll be packing houses, stockyards and factories for hides, tallow and other cattle by-products. Local sheep will produce more wool than in all areas between Nueces County and Mexico combined.'

It could happen. Jim had seen sheepmen in town. They ran small flocks in narrow valleys between the burning hills to the north and east of Palmito. They kept their own company, drinking in a scruffy cantina in the Mexican section, loafing on its porch and eyeing the *señoritas*. When they'd driven themselves crazy with lewd fantasizing, they would pool their money, throw dice, and the winner would come to the Gulf Trader and repair upstairs with one or other of Lena-Marie's small team of working girls.

Jim had also seen why it had been impossible for the Yankees to starve out the Texans. Longhorn cattle abounded in the coastal lands, congregating wherever the grass was rich. But coming off this sour country, many had big heads and over-developed horns. They were also very wild. Approach them and they would spring up, raising their shaggy heads and bellowing outrage at the intrusion of horse and man, then gallop off a half-mile in bunched, jostling disorder, wide 'handlebars' a-clacking.

Meantime, the wealth the cattle might one day constitute was untapped, though groups of range riders like himself drifted in, assessing the possibilities.

The Mexicans went on fishing, their womenfolk

mending the nets and the men setting to sea in creaking boats with small, much-patched sails.

Jim's duties were not onerous, though some were new to him. Coastal trading vessels brought in goods like bananas and other produce from Mexico. He was required to help in the unloading of their cargoes and the freighting of them by wagons or teams of pack mules to the sparse settlements of the semi-arid Gulf Coastal Plain, the undeveloped port's prospective hinterland. He could see no large profits in the work he did, but he trusted the Baptistes knew what they were about.

Discreetly, he pursued enquiries about Woodson Waldrop. No one knew anything, or so they said. Jim couldn't press the matter too diligently. In frontier places, a man's past was his past and the code was you didn't try to dig it up. The business of the fight on the day of his arrival still rankled, too. He wasn't apt to become a bosom pal of any of Woody's crowd in a hurry.

Finally, and purely by fortune, casual self-introductions with a crewman from one of the boats from Mexico put him somewhere near getting on the track of what he wanted to know.

The man's name was Tomas Vasquez and they were in a seafront *cantina*. Jim was drinking Mexican beer and the sailor had brought his mug of thick black coffee and plate of stacked *tortillas*, fried eggs and *frijoles* to share the table by the dirty window overlooking the jetty.

'You can call me Tomas, señor, because I observe you are no amigo to Woo-dee.'

'Woodson Waldrop? You know him?'

'But of course. I once rode with his gang. During the late war, *señor*.'

Jim's interest was grabbed. 'Drop the señor – I'm Jim. And I'd like to know more. How do you know I'm not Woody's friend?'

Tomas was an older man, in his forties, with a thickening waistline and grizzled beard and hair. He scratched his stomach abstractedly.

'You never work on the night shift, Jim.'

Jim was aware that on dark nights, when the sea fog descended on the coast, Woody Waldrop and his most trusted sidekicks rowed out into the clammy darkness to rendezvous with ships that came and went unseen. In his room above the Gulf Trader, he'd hear above the ever-present murmur of the waves on the beach a muffled, semi-distant squeal of pulleys, the clankings and quiet thuds of secret activity.

He'd guessed what the work was: the transfer of mysterious, illicit cargoes from ship to shore, and maybe shore to ship. Whatever the Baptistes were up to these days, it wasn't primarily importing bananas. But tensions were high enough already that he didn't ask questions.

Jim nodded. 'Smuggling, you mean,' he said warily to Tomas. 'Contraband goods. The Baptistes are past masters at it from the war years.'

'That is one part of it.'

'What would be the rest?'

'Passage for immigrants. Sometimes unwilling immigrants and usually girls.'

Jim was only mildly surprised. The girls who worked at the saloon for Lena-Marie came and went in what he was beginning to see as a regular procession. The prettiest and youngest were foreign, of Mexican or more obscure colour and origin.

He remembered aloud one of Waldrop's recent expeditions on which he hadn't been included.

'Woody, two of his cronies and a visiting German man recently took a covered wagon filled with an uncommonly large group of female arrivals to San Antonio, where it was said they were going into service,' he told Tomas. 'The men were all plenty eager to make the trip. They said somebody had to oblige the girls sooner or later and it might as well be them.'

'The girls would not have had a good time,' Tomas said sombrely. 'Somewhere along the lonely trail the unfortunates were prob'ly turned out of the wagon and raped. For the virgins – if any were intact after their sea voyage – it would have been a cruel education. Rolled in the dust and deflowered amidst the screams of their companions and the ribaldry of their escorts; dirtied and blooded for new lives. You see, Jim amigo, the service that awaits these girls in the big towns is not domestic service with charming families, as they have been promised, but prostitution in a cat house or hog farm.'

Jim wasn't green and he'd suspected this might have been the case. Society regarded prostitution as a dishonourable profession for American girls but fitting for females of other nationalities. Nonetheless, he felt sorry for the girls. At this time, prostitutes were scattered in growing thousands across the continent, from New Orleans to San Francisco. Most of them were immigrants, from poor families, often unable to speak English and reckoned inferior because of race, creed or colour.

He sighed. 'We can't reform the world, Tomas. I figure whoring is ineradicable. Maybe these girls are born to their fate.'

Tomas wrapped the last piece of egg in a tortilla and scoffed – both the food and at Jim.

'But what, amigo, if I was to tell you these things happen also to *norteamericano* women – Anglos as white as yourself?'

'I guess some make that choice. This is a free country now, we're told. Black, Indian, white . . . everyone.'

'You don't understand, Jim. I speak of women who are drugged and abducted and shipped from here – from Palmito – to Mexico and other countries where white flesh commands a price.'

'White slavery?' he said, astonished. 'I don't believe it.'

'It is happening under your nose. Girls come, but girls also go, taken out from the Palmito hotel at night to the big sailing ships by Woody and his gang.'

Jim felt hot and uncomfortable.

'You know Waldrop works for the Baptistes. Lena-Marie is my friend. I'll speak to her about what you say. I'm sure you've got it wrong. The traffic is likely innocent. These white women who go are probably fleeing willingly from abusive husbands, hardship or political discrimination. The Reconstruction maybe. . . . Leastways, I'm sure that's what Lena-Marie must believe. For a fact, as a madam she's good to her own girls and never forces them into the upstairs work.'

'Lena-Marie has the wool pulled over her eyes, I think,' Tomas said. 'I am certain she also does not know that Woody has always been a killer without conscience, scruple or loyalty.'

Jim found it easy to agree. 'So I tried to tell the Baptistes, but they wouldn't believe my story. They said it was mistaken identity when I told 'em he killed a harmless old Texan ranch-hand in the Trinity Creek country during the war. And I had no evidence or witness to prove otherwise, damnit.'

Surprisingly, Tomas laughed, but Jim quickly understood it was a bark of sarcasm.

'Hah! It was no mistake when Woody Waldrop shot down men on his own side in cold blood. For this I saw myself, serving in his militia. Would Señorita Baptiste, the lioness of the Confederacy, also dismiss the deaths of an entire Southern Army patrol at the hands of her good Woody? It was reason enough for me to quit his band and return to Old Mexico. For who could ride the river with such a man?'

Jim felt his pulse quicken. Hope glimmered in his heart. If Waldrop had slaughtered Confederate soldiers, and Lena-Marie was to be convinced of it by a disaffected member of his company, he thought it very possible she might give credence to his own claim that the gang leader had been no patriot but a ruthless, amoral killer who needed to be brought to justice.

'Tell me the whole story,' he said.

More than ever, Jim was determined not to rest until he had avenged Old Walt Burridge.

7

BETRAYAL UNDER THE STARS

Tomas Vasquez told a tale of deceit and treachery from the days when he'd been part of Waldrop's irregular militia company. Their job had been freighting arms smuggled across the border from Mexico through the Union army's cordon to embattled Confederate forces.

Cunning as a fox, Waldrop hit on what he thought was a clever plan. Shortly prior, they'd ambushed a small detachment of Union cavalry that had strayed unwittingly into territory not familiar to its leaders. For the guerrillas, it had been just like potting clay pigeons, and the encounter had put them in possession of a quantity of blue uniforms stripped from the bodies of their foes.

'It's a cinch, men. We'll kit ourselves out as bluebellies and drive the wagons straight through their lines.'

Tomas protested. 'Woody, this is terrible foolishness. Suppose we are challenged? It is a risky ruse.'

'Aw, leave off bellyachin', Vasquez. That's the trouble with you greasers – no grit. Are you comin' with us or are you quittin'?'

Tomas, to whose Latin temperament honour and chivalry made a strong appeal, wanted no truck with going under false colours, but walking away from Waldrop's roughneck bunch and maybe collecting a bullet in the back for a principled stand made no sense either. Reluctantly, he gave his approval.

'Very well. I don't like it, I have a real bad feeling – but I will come, gringo.'

Waldrop tipped Tomas's hat off his head. 'That's *Mister* Gringo to you!'

When Tomas stooped to pick up his headgear, Waldrop kicked him in his ample rear and the rest of the men hooted derisively as he stumbled forward and went down on all fours.

Waldrop said pontifically, 'Your greaser is made up of equal parts of 'magination, superstition an' fear. Gonna lick my boots, Vasquez?'

Tomas wasn't, but he was obliged to swallow his pride.

The boss having had his fun, the gang rode north in its ill-fitting Yankee garb, escorting the two wagons packed with a shipment of guns and ammunition intended for General Richard Taylor's hard-pressed army in Louisiana.

By a quirk of fate, it wasn't bluecoats who spotted

them fording a river but a patrol of grey-clad horse-men. The riders gave vent to the spine-chilling, Rebel-yell war whoop of the Southern armies and rode down on them.

Possibly they judged this badly outfitted Union company with its lumbering supply wagons would be easy pickings, cowed immediately by their show of strength and speed. They weren't to know they were up against ruthless, mercenary scum long versed in the villainy of the outlaw trail.

'*Caramba!*' Tomas moaned. 'They think we are their enemies in our blue coats. They will shoot us dead!'

'Into the shallows and the willows, fellers!' Waldrop hollered. 'Take cover an' pick your targets!'

'*Madre de Dios*, Woody!' Tomas cried. 'They are Southern cavalry. Do you mean for us to kill our *compadres?*'

Waldrop laughed maliciously, as though he took delight in the prospect of a bloody clash, regardless of its fatal absurdity for what was their own side.

'It's them or us, greaser! They don't know who we are, 'cept we're in bluebelly uniforms. They'll wipe us out less'n we fight back.'

He levered a round into the chamber of his rifle and fired on the Confederate patrol's leader who, at a distance of about 200 yards, was coming in fast.

The soft bullet took the captain in the shoulder, making mincemeat of an area about six inches in diameter. He was pitched from the saddle into the shallows, instantly producing a swirl of red in the turning waters. He didn't get to his feet.

70

Gallant and undaunted, his men opened return fire as they stormed in along the edge of the river. A fusillade of shots thudded into the willows and the wagons. Splinters, green and white, flew. A bullet hit a horse and it screamed before going down, thrashing and splashing wildly.

With shrieks of rage and defiance, the bluecoat imposters poured a withering hail of slugs into the mounted attackers from their sheltered positions. Tomas pleaded.

'Stop it, Woody! Stop it! They are our friends—'

'*Shut up, yuh ol' goat*! We gotta wipe 'em out now.'

Horrified, Tomas burst bravely into the open.

'Stop shooting! We are not the enemy. We are for the Southerners!'

But it was too late. Not a single Confederate saddle still carried a man. Only one trooper was still alive and when he made a break for it on foot, Waldrop callously shot him in the back.

'This stays our secret, boys. If one man lives to tell a tale, we chance our profits. An' I don't have to tell yuh, we give up payment in gold for nothin' nor nobody.'

Tomas had no option but to keep his trap shut, or share death with the rash Confederate patrol. If he'd run, he, too, would have died with his heels up.

At the first opportunity, he had quit his disgusting companions and took refuge in Matamoros.

Jim was staggered once he'd heard Tomas's story and knew the full extent of Woodson Waldrop's crimes. But he recognized Tomas's testimony could be of

71

value in bringing the hook-nosed killer to a reckoning in a land beyond any law other than the Baptistes and their shady business friends with fine plans for Palmito's future.

When Jim had met Lena-Marie in Brownsville, she had been to outward appearances a saloon girl and bar-room singer. He'd discovered she was, in truth, a born, strong-willed leader, working undercover for the cause of the Confederacy and taking initiatives in an arena where women did not readily win power. She was a mistress of all kinds of situations and knew how to weave a web of deception. But Jim also knew she didn't tolerate guile used against herself and expected loyalty to her interests from those she engaged.

With the war over, she'd not allowed life to pall for herself or her brother and was deeply into new enterprises arising and benefiting from her singular talents.

Through Tomas, Lena-Marie might be made to see that Waldrop was untrustworthy. Jim felt sure that with Waldrop exposed as failing to meet her standards – intent on his own grubby agendas – the Baptistes' support for him would be withdrawn. Once he was rejected from their influential circle, isolated, the way would be clear for Jim to force a showdown without the retribution rebounding on himself.

Suppressing his excitement, Jim put his suggestion to Tomas.

'It isn't too late to make Woody pay for what he did then. It's plain you plumb hate his guts, like I do.

Why not let's tell what you know to Señorita Baptiste? I can arrange a meeting while you're here in Palmito, so you can put it in your words, exactly, and answer any questions. She doesn't abide folks who fool her.'

'But what good will this do?'

'She'll do more than smack Woody's face; she'll dump him.'

'So? I am one helpless Mexican seaman. I do not have the courage to fight Waldrop. What is so wonderful in what you say?'

'It means I'd be free to go up against the louse and make him pay.'

Despite the sultry, salty heat, Tomas shivered.

'I don't know,' he said, a tremble in his voice. 'That is, I understand all that you say, *amigo mio*, but I smell trouble in it. . . .'

'Trouble for Woody! He's been playing a mighty dangerous game all along. I'll get that rotten, back-shooting, yellow hound if it's the last thing I do!'

Tomas swallowed the last of his cooled coffee. Pondered.

Slowly, his expression changed from wavering uncertainty to grim outrage as he remembered once more the affronts he'd suffered and the infamy of Waldrop's conduct.

Jim said nothing more to fire up the Mexican, but waited hopefully for his native passion to bubble to the surface.

'*Sí*! You are right,' he said at last, and his brown eyes flashed. He leaned forward to grab up Jim's hand and shake it. 'There is much honour in the Señorita Lena-Marie, I think, and she will know what

73

to do . . . to make the *híbrido* pay. I will go to visit with her, if and when this can be arranged.'

Jim's spirits soared. 'It can! And I'll fix it damn quick.'

Later, at the first opportunity, he found the Baptistes, sister and brother, together in the office at the rear of the Gulf Trader. He broached the matter striving to contain his eagerness.

Lena-Marie listened, watching him with dark and speculative eyes.

'I'd best leave the detail to Tomas Vasquez,' Jim said in a low, controlled voice. 'I know you think I've got a shuck in my snoot over Woody Waldrop, but he's got it coming when the beans are spilled.'

Raoul had a doubting, faintly sardonic grin on his face.

'These Mexicans! They have a busy lip . . . imagine all kinds of stuff. I'll bet he'll change his tune, or fail to show.'

Jim stiffened. 'I don't think Señor Vasquez was lying, Raoul. Waldrop seems to have you folks blink-ered.'

Lena-Marie put in quietly, 'Easy, Jim. We know Woody has a past. Most of the men I've ever employed have had that. It comes with our territory, I'm afraid. The form is not to pry.'

'But that doesn't mean we don't have the straight of it,' Raoul said smoothly. 'Woody is one of life's natural scoundrels, nothing worse. He comes from a simple, hardworking Texan family. He kicked over the traces in his youth, and a term of imprisonment for housebreaking at an impressionable age left him with grievances; also wise in the ways of criminals – a talent we've directed into worthy channels.'

'Sure . . .' Jim said scathingly. 'He's gotten himself the name of a bad man to tangle with. Very useful. And he's recruited a crowd of dubious ruffians, ready to rustle, rob and kill howsoever he orders. I say you're playing with fire.'

The Baptistes exchanged looks but refrained from denying the charge. In fact, a date was arranged for them to hear what Tomas had to tell.

'Secret meetings at night . . . very melodramatic, I'm sure, and probably quite unnecessary,' Raoul murmured.

This time, it was Jim's turn to bite his tongue.

When he was leaving, Lena-Marie placed a hand on his arm.

'Oh, Jim, don't take this so badly. We know Waldrop heads a tough crew, but such fellows are necessary to achieve our ends. I'm sure Raoul knows what's going on, but I will listen to what your Tomas Vasquez has to say.'

Jim sighed. 'Yeah . . . well, all right then, but I don't think you'll be talking so friendly about Waldrop after you've heard the story.'

Raoul determinedly put in the last word. 'That's if this Mex keeps the appointment and my sister believes him, of course.'

Jim Hunter took up a position on the narrow promontory of rock that stretched out to sea forming one arm of the bay which contained Palmito's waterfront. It was some minutes short of eleven. The lapping water shimmered in the starlight. Visibility was good, but not as clear as on a moonlight night.

He hoped the degree of darkness would suit Tomas Vasquez. The schooner he crewed on was a dark silhouette, sails furled, bobbing on the gentle swell of unbroken water several hundred yards distant from the shore. Not being under way, it was showing no running lights.

Tense minutes crept by. No movement showed on the Mexican vessel. Out in the bay, the silence and stillness were oppressive.

Behind him, Jim heard a scuffle of light, fast-moving footsteps. He drew back and crouched among the rocks. But it was only a ragamuffin Mexican boy, skipping purposefully toward him.

'Señor Hunter? Are you here? Where are you?'

A few gulls, disturbed by the intrusion, rose from their perches with a flap of wings and harsh, indignant cries.

Jim was puzzled, but the boy looked harmless and alone, so he showed himself.

'What is it, kid?'

'Message from Tomas, *señor*. He cannot come tonight, but perhaps tomorrow. . . .'

His information delivered, the boy sped back in the direction he'd come, and Jim quickly lost sight of him in the darkness and the jumbled rocks.

He cursed under his breath. He hadn't expected Vasquez to let him down, but it seemed Raoul was right after all. These Mexicans were a law unto themselves.

What was he to do?

The best plan he could think of was to go to Lena-Marie punctually but alone, tender apologies and hope she'd be agreeable to a rescheduling of the meeting.

His mind made up that this was the only course, he lit the bull's-eye lantern he'd brought with him and used its light to hurry himself back to the town and the humiliating task of breaking the news to the Baptistes.

To seaward, scant minutes after he'd left, a light winked from the dark bulk of the schooner. Going unanswered, it was repeated . . . then, regardless of the lack of response, followed by the detachment of a smaller blob of blackness from the outline of the greater.

Oars dipped and splashed phosphorescently in the darkness.

Tomas Vasquez rowed the dinghy to shore, perplexed by Jim's failure to show a light as he had promised. Well, maybe it was no nevermind. He could see well enough by starlight and the fewer signs for inquisitive folk to notice the better. He shuddered as he thought of what Waldrop and his gang would do to him if they thought their one-time compadre was about to split on them.

The small boat travelled length by length through the calm water, the gentle waves chuckling along its sides. The closer he came to the rocky shore, the more nervous he grew. He could see no sign of Jim Hunter and a premonition of impending disaster gnawed at his vitals.

He manoeuvred the row-boat into a steeply shelving beach in the lee of a rocky outcrop. Small pebbles and sand crunched under its stern. He pulled in and stowed the oars.

'Señor Jim?' he said quietly, but no one answered.

Maybe he was early or the Texan cowboy had been delayed. But they had both given their word, shaken hands on the arrangement. Despite his unease, Tomas felt he could not turn the boat around and row straight back whence he had come. He jumped out and waded calf-deep in his boots through the gently breaking water. As he climbed up on to the rocks, he heard a rustle and saw movement behind some bushes.

He knew immediately that this was not right. He leaped back to the beach just in time to see second and third shadowy figures emerge from a cleft in the rocks beyond the row-boat a piece. He turned and began to run as fast as his feet would carry him through the soft sand of the beach north of the bay.

The men didn't call out to him to stop. They pursued him silently except for the pounding of their feet and the harshness of their breathing. Any moment, he expected a shot to crash out and topple him. It didn't come and a chill ran down his exposed back. These men aimed to hunt him down and destroy him like hounds – but soundlessly so none should hear the deed.

'Who are you?' he cried through sobbing breaths of his own. 'Why are you following me? Leave me alone!'

Relentlessly, they were closing in on his heels. The

sand was heavy going, the toes of his boots sinking into it deeply, covering and uncovering them with each step. He took to rockier ground further from the water, the breath now starting to rasp in his throat.

The tactic allowed him to put on a burst of speed and widen the gap. Fear lent him wings. It also proved his undoing. A loose stone turned under his right foot. He felt a wrench at his ankle – a twist. Helpless to avoid it, he went down, sprawling.

As he rose, the weight he put on his right leg sent a bolt of agony through him. Limping, he set off again doggedly. But the foremost of his pursuers was on him now: bearded, hook-nosed and showing his teeth in a gratified snarl. Woody Waldrop!

Waldrop launched himself at Tomas, who dodged his plunge, stepped in and punched with all his strength. Waldrop was checked with a snort of rage. Tomas knew he was fighting for his life and got in another glancing blow to the hook nose, but it cost him his painful footing as Waldrop turned defensively to one side, letting Tomas's momentum carry him forward, stumbling.

Waldrop laughed harshly. 'So goin' to sea has made yuh kinda *salty*, huh?'

His hand went to his hip and he drew a bowie knife. It was wickedly sharp, thirteen inches long, sharpened only on one side to the curve of the tip, then sharpened on both sides to the point. The steel glinted blue-white in the starlight.

Tomas hit the ground in a heap and Waldrop dropped on top of him, both knees thumping into his back and pinning him. Waldrop grabbed his hair and pulled back his head, arching his throat. Then he slashed with the knife. He had a firm grip of the fearsome weapon with his hand up against a cunningly designed brass handguard that permitted him to exert maximum pressure and control.

The sharp blade sliced through skin, flesh, bone and vein. Blood spurted freely and copiously in all directions from the deep wound.

Mercifully, Tomas died very quickly, gagging on the blood from his slit throat.

Waldrop got up, wiping the redly wet knife on the Mexican's shirt and the back of his hand under his nose. The prominent feature was puffed and showing signs of bleeding.

'Asshole landed one!' he cussed. 'But he got his. Tie a rock to the pig's carcass, boys, and take it out to the deep water. Capsize his boat in the bay.'

8

SINNING IN TRINITY CREEK

Matt Harrison picked at the supper his wife had prepared for him. Finally, he made a clatter throwing down the fork when the meal was less than half-eaten, and left to go sit on the porch.

'I ain't hungry,' he stated grumpily.

Alice Harrison had hoped Jim Hunter's departure from the Double H might set things right; that her tormented heart might heal; that she'd be free to enjoy life and love with her rancher husband.

Experience, of which she learned she had very little in this regard, proved otherwise.

The problem, she was sure, stemmed not from her own response to Jim's leaving but from Matt's. He wasted long hours in a rocker on the porch, working his way through jugs of whiskey that didn't lift his melancholy or improve his bleak humour.

Matt had changed.

His heart was no longer in the job of reviving the Double H and unfairly he seemed to blame her for Jim's defection. Matt and Jim had been friends a long time. Ridiculously, it had taken not a war but a peace to split them. In a way, it would have been better if Jim had never returned from the war that had changed so much. Then she wouldn't have lost them both.

For Matt was indeed lost to her and everything except the dubious comfort of hard liquor.

Jim she'd now lost twice. Once, when he'd chosen to fight with Confederacy guerrillas, his strict whereabouts and fate unknown other than that the latter might easily be assumed to have been death. The second time, when he'd ridden out to rejoin his erstwhile, suspect friends on the coast.

Jim was out of her reach and she could do nothing for him. Her husband was a different matter. She felt it a duty that she should try to reclaim him before it was too late. But reasoning with him had already produced no meaningful result.

She determined the only thing she could do now to rescue him from the pernicious and growing influences of drink and self-pity was to deliver a sharp shock. It was a last resort and for herself it would mean swallowing her pride and demeaning herself in the leering eyes of Trinity Creek.

And there was no time like the present for a bull-by-the-horns approach, before she lost her simmering anger and her courage.

Taking off her apron, taking a deep breath, she

went out on to the porch and placed her hands on her hips.

'Put down that whiskey, Matt Harrison, and listen up!' she declared. 'I'm sick of your cantankerousness, your laziness and your insobriety! Through with it! I'm leaving you until you come to your senses, you understand?'

Matt's jaw dropped stupidly. He tried to fix her with glassy eyes.

'Uhh? What is this, honey? Leaving me ...? Where will you go? Why?'

'You know full well why. I've told you a thousand times already.'

'S-sure.' He belched fumily. 'Nag, nag, nag, as if things ain't bad enough.'

Alice turned her pretty face in disgust. Her colour was high and her voice shook.

'This time I've got a carpetbag packed and I'm riding the buckboard to town. You can pick it up from the livery. Me, you'll find at the Settlers' Hotel. I'll charge the cost of a room to the Double H's account. They can add it to your whiskey bill. Lord knows, we'll go broke one way or another, and you'll lose the ranch unless you see sense fast.'

Alice put her trust in her knowledge that Matt was not a vicious man. He wouldn't resort to violence to stop her, even when inebriated.

Dumbfounded, he let her go. When he was sober, she hoped he would feel bad about having virtually driven her out with his moods and his drunkenness.

But she couldn't help a feeling of guilt herself. Should she have ever married Matt? Had her motives been no more than a grasp at the only security on offer in a troubled time?

Word soon spread around Trinity Creek that Matt Harrison's bride, attractive young former school ma'am Alice Cornhill, was back in town, renting a fifty-cents-a-day back room at the hotel. It was the kind of burg where the gossips watched and never missed a thing. And Alice was unmissable by any place's yardstick. Her flowing fair hair, blue eyes and clear complexion made her a picture. She had no fat on her frame either, though marriage had somehow filled out the right places to an exciting perfection.

Sniffy matrons barely acknowledged her on the street. Men with time on their hands sucked their teeth at workplace and other windows. All observed the passing-by of her unescorted figure with low growls of disapproval at the challenge her desirability presented but her status disallowed anyone to take up.

' 'Tain't right,' was a common conclusion. 'A good woman's place is with her man, keepin' house and makin' babies.'

Alice's successor at Alexander McAuley's private schoolroom, the insolent but accommodating Miss Ruby Smith, discussed the matter with him for whom she acted doubly as a mistress – in schoolroom and bed-chamber – testing out his reaction and the reliability of her own position.

'Well, who would have thought it? Seems plain to me – Mrs Snooty ain't such a goody-goody after all. She must be looking for mischief, setting up and sleeping away from home in that there hotel room. Never could trust a prig, could you?'

McAuley, having supported the Union throughout the late conflict, had prospered under the new conditions of the Reconstruction. His mercantile store and real estate interests managed to suck up a tidy percentage of whatever money was spent in town. For a man who'd started out as a storekeeper, he cut a fine sartorial figure. No woollen work shirt and coarse pants for him, he was outfitted in a suit of imported worsted cloth – expertly tailored to conceal a swelling paunch – a velvet vest and a carefully knotted tie. His regular daily visit to the barbershop kept him looking smooth and sleek and smelling of expensive pomade supplied by his own emporium.

He scoffed dismissively at Ruby Smith's unspoken fears.

'Alice Cornhill should never have left her post with me and married an uncouth cowpuncher. The woman is pathetic . . . a little nobody.'

But what he said was not what he thought.

McAuley's success in business was based in large measure on his talent for masking the devious workings of a quick mind. Duplicity, therefore, came to him with practised ease. A little hypocrisy could often turn a big profit. Likewise, his political sympathies had been placed with acumen rather than sincerity, making him an influential force in affairs of local administration and giving him the confidence he could take anything he wanted.

Ruby was reassured by his adamant verdict on her forerunner as his offspring's teacher. She didn't demur as he abstractedly unhooked and unlaced her dress. They were in the front parlour of the cottage he'd once rented to the Cornhills and she'd already removed the severe smock she wore for her schoolroom duties. She knew McAuley wasn't visiting as her landlord or employer. She also knew it was high time to fix his abstraction – occasioned perhaps by reflections about pretty Alice – with distraction.

'Here, let me,' she said, and took off frock and petticoats in a trice. In the world she'd lived in, you kept the advantage and your comforts by letting the men who had the power take just enough of what they wanted to keep them returning for more.

McAuley filled his eyes with her bounty, now provocatively attired in only a crêpe chemise, openwork black silk stockings and drawers of the finest lawn. The drawers were magnificent, edged with rich Valenciennes lace and decorated at the sides with red satin bows.

She commented with an arch sauciness, 'Why, I do believe you ain't stiff as a rolling-pin.'

Without prompting, she turned and leaned forward over the couch, feet well apart and putting her chin on her arms which she folded on top of its cushioned back.

McAuley raised the chemise and turned it up over her shoulders, then his practised fingers reached for the buttons of her drawers. But all the time he was thinking what extraordinarily large hips and thighs she had; how rampantly luxuriant was the growth of black hair already peeking through the drawers' open slit. . . .

'Get 'em undone, lover,' she said, shooting a suitably imploring look at him over her shoulder. 'I do declare this gal is on fire for her drawers to fall to the south!'

Ruby's familiar charms were temptingly luscious. She had to be the greatest libertine McAuley had ever met with, but today he hankered anew to down the drawers and reveal the altogether daintier moons of a young lady who did not share Ruby's coarseness and would never dream of offering herself to him with such brazen forwardness.

Mrs Alice Harrison's return to town and lodging at the hotel was an unexpected development. McAuley's conjectures about what it meant, what it offered in the way of opportunity to satisfy his old lusts grew ever wilder as the days passed.

Whatever the young woman's reasons for living in town, away from her husband, he was determined to have her for himself. Ruby Smith had outlived her novelty. It was high time to send her packing. Perhaps the coveted Alice would be amenable to reinstatement as his children's schoolteacher on terms she'd once rejected.

After all, he argued to himself optimistically, she was no longer a chaste and silly virgin. She'd been living for months as the only female on a ranch far from any neighbours. Her boorish husband's old partner had rejoined him only temporarily. Without let or hindrance, Harrison would have been a weak fool not to have used her vigorously.

Thus Alexander McAuley convinced himself Alice

Harrison had been obliged to perform wifely duties of a kind that would have moderated previously uncooperative and prudish attitudes. Also, that her presence in town meant she would be ready after a spell of hardship and abstinence to lend a different ear to his overtures.

'No two ways about it – I'll have her,' he grunted.

Beside him, Ruby Smith propped herself up on an elbow, letting the sheets slip from her generous and naked bosom. She plumped a pillow of the bed they shared without the sanction of matrimony.

'What did you say, Alex dear?'

'Uh – nothing, Ruby. Thinking aloud is all.'

In point of fact, having failed to get full satisfaction from Ruby's compliant body, he had just perfected in his mind plans for the realization of his dreams concerning the unconsciously teasing Mrs Alice Harrison.

9

BUSHWHACKER'S
TRAP

Jim Hunter had no illusions. He knew life in the corner of Texas containing Palmito was always eventful and frequently short. It was a dangerous and lawless land for the wariest. Nonetheless, he wasn't naïve. The apparent loss of Tomas Vasquez in a drowning accident was too hard to swallow. Thinking of how he'd been lured from the probable true scene of his informant's death filled Jim with cold fury.

He searched the 'dobe quarter of the seaside town high and low for the Mexican boy who'd brought the 'message from Tomas'. He found plenty of raggedy-assed urchins – in fact, a small army of wide-eyed children followed him around – but none he could identify as the one in question.

When he accused the fisherfolk of hiding the boy

he sought, they became surly or indignant. Outnumbered, he didn't care to try conclusions with them, though in his heart he knew they were lying when they protested they 'knew notheeng, señor'.

Lena-Marie and her brother told him bluntly he was wasting his free time. Maybe, they suggested, Tomas had staged his drowning himself and simply disappeared, unwilling or unable to back up his outrageous tale of wartime treachery.

Raoul offered the information that there were Mexicans among the sheepherders working the valleys to the north. Jim decided it might be a good idea to give the chestnut gelding stabled at the livery barn a run.

The town left behind, instinct warned him fast enough he was being followed, but the land rose and fell in a series of ripples and he couldn't glimpse the rider who, putting coincidence aside, had to be tracking him. The land was dry; the sky clear and blue. It would require no skill to follow the thin banner of dust he couldn't avoid raising. Indeed, the follower was creating one of his own that tended to confirm Jim's apprehensions.

Apart from four buzzards that rode the thermals high above, wheeling silently on spread black wings, nothing else moved in the stillness and the heat.

Mindful of Tomas Vasquez's fate, he kept careful watch on his backtrail. He didn't cotton to the notion of making a 'disappearance' of his own. But the mysterious shadower was playing clever and kept his distance.

Eventually, he came in sight of the first of the

dilapidated wooden shacks used by the sheepmen. It was backed by a grove of majestic sycamores that grew on a slope rising from the bottomland on the other side of a small creek, dapple-shadowed by the large, maple-like leaves of the trees.

Jim cast a glance over his shoulder. No sign of the rider who might be stalking him. The only sound of life was hoarse-voiced frogs croaking among the reeds of a boggy section of the far bank; the only movement, a hovering dragonfly. He let the chestnut stand, to dip his muzzle into the coolness of the fetlock-deep running water.

When the horse had drunk his fill, and lifted a dripping mouth and nose, Jim nudged with his knees and flicked the rein ends. To his surprise the horse balked, standing stock-still with ears pointing forward.

Jim laughed softly. 'C'mon, 'Nut, you ornery critter. It's just frogs. The trouble, if there's any, is coming up behind.'

With another backward look, he pushed again with his knees and kicked the horse's flanks with his heels. Even then – and though his familiar mount was usually a willing animal – the thought that danger might lie ahead didn't cross his mind. Frowning deeply, he was preoccupied with the puzzle of the elusive follower.

Ill at ease, the chestnut splashed across the shallow creek, stepping high and setting sparkling fountains of spray flying from his hoofs. Reaching the other bank in a sidestepping fashion, he stood quivering in every muscle. His eyes rolled wildly.

That was when the bushwhacker hidden in the shadowy timber ahead acted, and for a split-second Jim realized he'd been fooled. Real bad. For with all his attention on what might be happening behind him, he'd been tricked into riding into an obvious trap.

The shot rang out.

His hat went spinning away from his head just before he registered the flash and the vicious crack of the rifle in the timber. Agonizing, blinding pain tore through his head. He reeled from the saddle.

When he hit the water, hitting the stones under the surface with his shoulder, he rolled once. Then he didn't move.

The chestnut, ears still twitching, dance-stepped backwards from him.

After the ringing echoes of the single shot had died, silence resumed except for the lapping of the creek and the croaking of the frogs.

In the shadows of the timber, the bushwhacker gloated at the success of the plan to divert the victim's attention, and at the grim result of his hand-iwork.

'Sly,' he said.

He watched. A minute elapsed and the nervous chestnut gelding edged forward again, treading on dropped reins. The bronc poked its nose at the back of his prone rider's neck. A soft whinnying brought no response.

With a grin of triumph, the bushwhacker left his nest between the massive white, tan and brown trunks of the sycamores. His boots crunched on the accumulated debris of dropped leaves, twigs and fruit. It had been a hot, dry summer and the trees, which preferred deeply moist soil, were a mite stressed.

The rifleman walked through to the edge of a clearing where he'd hitched his horse to the undergrowth. He shoved the gun into the saddle scabbard, mounted up, and rode off.

He aimed to meet up with his partner in crime who'd aggravatingly – but wilily, misleadingly – dogged Jim Hunter from Palmito.

Alice Harrison had an almost feverish desire to escape Trinity Creek, but knew she couldn't.

Where would she go? Back to the cattle range and Matt? To the Gulf coast to find Jim Hunter?

The second thought brought immediate, guilty heat to her cheeks. She was married now and Jim's flirting ways were part of a past best forgotten. Moreover, it was an impractical course since she didn't know Jim's precise whereabouts any more than she had when he'd been away at war. She couldn't, *wouldn't* run off. Her place was here till Matt Harrison reformed his drunken ways, pulled himself together, and solved the difficult problem of making something of the Double H lone-handed.

So she scuttled along the town's boardwalks, trying to hide herself in her black cloak from what she imagined to be the accusing stares of the citizenry, especially the womenfolk who'd effectively ostracized her. People who'd known her for years walked right by her on the street without so much as exchanging a polite nod.

As quickly as she could, she returned to the hotel with her modest, essential purchases from McAuley's mercantile. In the stuffy lobby she was hailed by the desk clerk as she scooted for the stairs.

The clerk, whom she knew simply as Packham, was young, doughy-faced, pimply, impurely minded – and, at present, smirking.

'Oh, Mrs Harrison ma'am! You have a visitor.'

Her heartbeats quickened. Had Matt come to see her, to apologize for his unbearable behaviour and take her home?

'A visitor? Here?'

'Upstairs, ma'am. I took the *liberty* of lending him a key. I thought it *seemly*, him being a *respected gentleman* and all, and wishing *privacy*.'

Every other word was loaded with indecent insinuation. Nudges and winks could not have been more eloquent.

Alice was incredulous. 'You let someone into my room?'

'Oh, it wasn't a "someone", ma'am.' Packham lowered his voice conspiratorially. 'It was Mr Alexander McAuley himself, who, as you may know, holds a large mortgage on the hotel.'

Alice's face burned, not with embarrassment but with suppressed fury.

'I didn't know and I don't see your point. The room is rented to me! I shall send him away instantly.'

While the clerk shrugged at her indignation, Alice

went directly to the stairs. She couldn't think what her former employer and landlord could want with her, but she knew she wanted nothing with him.

She stormed into the small room to find the unwelcome visitor seated on the bed that dominated it.

'Mr McAuley! You've no right to be in here. You're at fault, sir! I must ask you to leave this moment.'

McAuley's ordinarily pale cheeks were flushed as though with excitement. He got to his feet, not to comply with her request, which he affected not to have heard, but to reach for her.

'Slip off your cloak and untie your bonnet, my dear. I've missed you in your long absence from town. While we talk, let your beautiful hair flow loose and free.'

Alice was alarmed by his manner. 'I shall do no such thing! We have nothing to talk about, Mr McAuley.'

'In that you're very wrong, missy,' McAuley said, hardening his tone. 'I've come to counsel you that the town finds your situation disagreeable to it – repugnant perhaps.'

Alice snorted at the silliness of what he was saying, though she'd experienced daily and unhappily the results of prejudiced gossip.

'What do you mean?' she asked, though the moment she had, she regretted it. She'd no doubt stories about the trouble between herself and Matt were in circulation among the maliciously tongued, but she'd also no wish to discuss them with the odious McAuley.

Animosity was everywhere in these difficult times. In particular, Texans who'd been dispossessed of their property and their loved ones resented the new precedence of the minority who'd supported the Union, which included Alexander McAuley and Matt Harrison. Matt owned cattle and land. Even though he was now struggling in his attempt to put his ranch back on its feet, some folk plainly resented him – and, by extension, her. As in any community, there were elements that, while having benefited in the past from the business of a ranch like the Double H, harboured envy and minor grudges. These were exacerbated by the complexities and irritations of the Reconstruction.

To put a foot wrong, to step outside normal conventions, gave the resentful a peg, however irrelevant, on which to hang their frustrations.

McAuley explained it, shaping the facts to his own ends.

'Folk don't take kindly to women living in – uh – unusual situations. Looking like she's having it easy when others of her standing must endure their unhappy lot. It's not acceptable.'

To herself, Alice conceded his point. It was one of the aspects she'd felt awkward about in the presence of others of her kind who merely visited town.

Ranch wives were expected to endure the primitive conditions, the scarcity of manufactured comforts and the long periods of loneliness, while they helped their men wrest a living from the raw land. It was part of their duty. The outdoor chores were a never-ending round. The wife's functions were to tend a garden patch, care for domestic live-stock, cook, clean the home, and bear her man's children. The beauty of youth quickly faded. Fair skin was weathered by the sun and wind, heat and cold, so that the look of old age came long before time. Some died of illness or in childbirth, or of the sheer, godawful drudgery in a harsh climate. Most survivors were dried-up, wrinkled crones.

McAuley expanded on his argument, oozing false sympathy.

'Of course, your mistake was in leaving my – uh – service and marrying a lowly rancher. Most of these small cattlemen are trash at bottom with nothing but the haziest conception of what it takes to run a real business – more conceit than ability. I understand your position completely. The abuse must have been awful—'

A flood of defensive, angry words spilled from Alice's lips.

'You do not understand my position, Mr McAuley! The land might be hard and pitiless for women, but Matt was an excellent choice of husband – a caring, decent man! But as you seem to know he has fallen on hard times. It's just that he's chosen a solution he must reconsider if he wishes to keep me on the Double H.'

'Ah, yes . . . it has been noticed Harrison has taken to – shall we say? – boozing it up. Demeaning. Terrible for a lady, I'm sure.'

'I can cope without your assumptions.'

'But not without my help and protection, Alice.' He took a deep breath. 'You know, I find it's you alone among earth's women I truly admire, and I have a proposition that you should return to me.'

'Thank you, but I want no school ma'am post, Mr McAuley,' she said firmly. 'Besides, I understand you have another – lady, in that situation.'

'Oh, Miss Smith could easily be dispensed with, my dear. You would be most welcome to fill her place *completely*. We could be most careful and discreet—'

'Not another word, sir!' Alice flared. 'Your suggestion is offensive. I'll be no man's hussy. My husband provides for me and we exchanged vows to be each other's until death do us part. Now get out!'

McAuley shook his head sadly.

'Well, well – that's a great pity, Mrs Harrison. I had a notion I might be better received. I hope you'll be brought to your good senses before it's too late. Else, mark my words, this thing will end in grief. . . .'

Alice was relieved when he stamped out without more ado. But she found herself left frightened and shaking. In her bones, she knew he wouldn't let the matter lie.

What did McAuley intend to do to bring her to her senses?

10

HAMMERWORK

Jim Hunter dared not move a muscle. Every advantage was with the bushwhacker hidden in the trees. In the open, in the shallows of the creek, he had no cover but a horse he couldn't afford to lose. If he made a move for his own long gun, or even his belt gun, he'd be picked off with a second round from the assassin's rifle before he could locate a target. All that was left to him was to make no move at all; to play possum and hope the marksman confidently assumed he'd killed him with a single shot.

It was a wonder he hadn't, Jim thought ruefully.

He lay perfectly still, letting the water saturate his clothes, fill his boots. The chestnut backed off after nuzzling his neck with a velvety wet nose. He guessed a horse's intelligence was of a different order in which no accounting existed for the strange ways of men. 'Nut whinnied in soft disapproval but wasn't particularly interested in the game.

Straining his ears above the soft chuckle of the stream, Jim shortly heard the crunch of the rifleman's boots as he moved away from his sniper's nest through the fallen, heat-dried sheddings of the sycamores common in this part of Texas. The crackles and rustles thankfully receded.

His attacker was anxious to be away from the scene – as well he might be, lest some other, inquisitive parties were drawn by the one, sudden rifle shot in sparsely populated country. The few inhabitants would be apt to know their neighbours' game-hunting habits and haunts; an unexpected shot could be a signal of trouble.

Shortly after, Jim thought he detected a distant pound of hoofs that quickly faded. Tentatively, he chanced raising his head and – praise be! – no bullet came. The would-be killer had ridden off, thinking his mission accomplished.

He got up. His head reeled and his shoulder was sore from its impact with the rocky creek bed, but he was alive and in one unbroken piece. The big-calibre slug that had removed his hat had also taken a chunk of hair and skin off his scalp. He retrieved the hat, poked a finger through the hole in the crown and pursed his lips in a sibilant whistle. Death had passed him close.

Everything confirmed Tomas Vasquez's disappearance hadn't been voluntary. Almost certainly, the Mexican was dead and his killer or killers were now out to stop him probing into the affair too deeply.

To Jim's mind, the murder and the attempt on his own life had to be the work of Woody Waldrop and his bunch, regardless of what his friends the Baptistes thought.

But how had the gang learned Tomas had been about to reveal the damning truth about their dastardly wartime slaughter of men who fought, as they supposedly did, for the South?

It seemed unlikely that Tomas would have been so foolish, or had the opportunity, to let slip word of the arranged meeting at which he was to have enlightened Lena-Marie.

Grimly, he moved toward inescapable conclusions.

Despite her contemptuous dismissal of him from her cramped and airless hotel room, Alexander McAuley still coveted Alice Harrison and was determined to have the fair-haired young beauty for himself.

He persuaded himself she'd encouraged his attention by abandoning her husband and coming to live in unorthodox fashion for a married lady in a cheap hotel room. Her protestations of undying faithfulness to her husband had to be a lie merely waiting for the opportunity to be proven. For a fact, the women of his experience were more practical and less romantic in such matters than men.

If only the miserable Matt Harrison could be removed from the equation, his wife would be ripe for picking by another, which he'd make sure was himself. He was one of the finest men in this part of Texas. She could have been the finest belle and had every luxury and his unstinting attention – every night, all night long! – had she stayed in his employ and not married a horny-handed cowpuncher.

It was still not too late. What he had to do was reduce Harrison to circumstances in which she'd realize he no longer, and never would, have the means to provide the masculine support that was a woman's prime need in a brutal land. Every female on the frontier was under constant siege, both from the elements and the disproportionate number of unattached males seeking an outlet for their instincts.

Harrison had played into McAuley's hands with his growing addiction to liquor. He'd been seen from time to time on Trinity Creek's streets sufficiently under its influence to raise serious doubts about his sanity.

McAuley set about putting around a malicious story that he told himself was liable to be the truth.

'Of course,' he said, 'propriety calls for a wife to be by her husband's side, not skulking in a hotel room alone and inviting of all manner of private mischief, but maybe the lady has just reason. In his drinking fits, Harrison abused and beat her black and blue till she feared for her very life. This is between me and you and the gate post, of course. . . .'

Alice had lived with her widowed mother in Trinity Creek for many years before her marriage. Pretty Miss Cornhill had been a popular figure. Many young men's hearts had been broken when she'd accepted Matt Harrison for a husband. Consequently, it wasn't too hard to discredit him. Willing tongues spread the rumours and bully-boys and riff-raff were soon open to the suggestion that sport could be had in bringing the once high-and-mighty rancher and ex-Union army captain to a reckoning.

Matt Harrison was asking for a comeuppance, wasn't he?

The day had passed and dusk was beginning to deepen into night. Matt Harrison tried to remember where he'd hitched the horse he'd ridden to town. It was high time he was making tracks back to the Double H. He'd spent some hours drinking and his pockets were empty of coin and the bottle he still clutched without realizing it held only dregs.

Considerably befuddled, and in blissful ignorance of the fact that he was being followed, he lurched into the black shadows of an alleyway where he had dimly formed intentions of relieving himself.

He fumbled one-handed with his pants while owlishly striving not to spill the wild mare's milk left in his bottle. He was incapable of appreciating the mishap was impossible without upending it.

Standing without moving as minutes passed, his ears caught the sounds of soft and stealthy movements yet failed to make sense of them. Shadowy figures blocked the narrow entries to the alleyway at both ends.

'Right, boys,' a voice grated. 'Fix the loco sonofabitch!'

Matt squinted his eyes and peered into the darkness. He wasn't so snooze-marooed as to think he was a-hearing owls and a-seeing elephants. Foreboding stirred in him. These were men – and they meant him nothing but harm. They had the smell of pure poison.

But his reactions were way too slow.

They came at him in a rush. Escape ahead and behind was blocked off. He got the closest wall at his back and swung his whiskey bottle in an ineffective arc. Impact with a raised arm tore it from his grip and it exploded at his feet into tinkling shards.

Blows rained on his shoulders, his head, and into his face. Pain paradoxically cleared his head a mite and his anger mounted. He was outnumbered, hopelessly.

'Damn you!' he snarled. 'This is no fair fight. What's your gripe, you yellow-livered scum?'

A right hook slammed into his mouth, bloodying his lips, breaking teeth and stopping further talk. No sooner did he whirl in one direction to fend off a blow, or deliver a retaliatory punch of his own, than he was hit from another.

He reeled, fighting to keep his feet, and there was no backing off. He was trapped on all sides by the walls of the alley and a pack of cowards.

He figured some of his attackers were people he knew – store clerks, a saloon swamper, a stable hand, local layabouts. They surrounded him and punched and pummelled him to and fro between them. Like himself, they'd been drinking. They were flushed, but ugly with it.

No one deigned to answer his question as to their motives, but when he stepped back on to a piece of wet and broken glass that slid under his foot causing him to lose his balance and fall, they roared approval.

'Git the boot in!' someone howled.

The kicks came hard and fast to body and head. Matt felt at least one of his ribs crack. He screamed in pain. He was down and his lights were about to be snuffed out.

Desperately, he flung his arms around one of the attacker's legs and toppled him. As the man fell, his head hit the alley wall with the thud a thrown water-melon might make and he crumpled limply into the trash and the glass.

In the rapidly gathering darkness, more of the mob stumbled over their prostrate companion, and Matt was able to lurch up to make an unsteady stand.

He managed a commendably powerful left swing that mashed the nose of an assailant accidentally elbowed into his fist's path by a crowding accom-plice. Curses and blood flowed freely.

But a fresh opponent stepped in close to hammer Matt's sore ribs with a left, a right, then a left again. He was winded and doubled over. Then an uppercut to his jaw straightened him in time to bring his head up to meet the hard iron of a gun held by its barrel and swung from behind.

A cascade of light burst in his swimming brain only to be absorbed by a dense, stifling fog. Matt went down again, but this time he was unconscious before he hit the ground.

The assailant whose head had hit the wall and who'd been trampled over got to his knees, groan-ing. He retched and then vomited.

'Oh Gawd, I think I'm gonna die.' He clutched his head in both hands.

'Shit . . . reckon the bastard's busted Jeb's head,' another of the mob said. 'He's gotta pay for that!'

Someone had brought along a blacksmith's hammer and saw a chance to put it to use, regardless that the savage beating was done and Matt was beyond fight or feeling.

'Sure he'll pay,' he said. 'He won't be no tough range-boss an' wife-beater with broken kneecaps.'

The hammer rose and fell. The sound of breaking bone was a chilling sound, but these men were in a hot sweat of excitement, impervious to the excess of pain, anguish and torment they were storing up for their senseless victim.

Too, their ringleaders had secretly been promised money if the job was done well, which helped make minds easier when vicious zeal got out of hand.

Scant minutes later, they left Matt lying motionless in the blood-spattered dust of the alleyway. He remained out to the world, but his face was screwed up and feverish squeaks of nightmare agony were blubbering through his wetly broken lips.

Alice Harrison overheard the gossip going around town about the crippling of her husband only many days later. She rushed immediately to the house and surgery of the Trinity Creek medico.

The place was large for Trinity Creek with a second storey and a garden enclosed by a white picket fence. A neatly lettered sign proclaimed the residence to be that of John G. Brandon, MD, late of Edinburgh and Boston.

But Matt wasn't there.

Doc Brandon, an elderly man with white hair and a brusque manner, told Alice Matt had insisted on being returned to his ranch to recuperate.

'His right kneecap was the worst,' he said with the matter-of-factness of a sawbones who'd lately witnessed at first hand the barbarities of war. 'Shattered. This causes great pain and is practically impossible to remedy, as it is difficult to remove all of the splintered bone. From this day forth, your husband will never walk without a limp.'

Tears formed in Alice's eyes but she swallowed and didn't let them spill.

'They must have been vermin who did it!'

Brandon harrumphed. 'Some say it was done in your behalf – on account of your husband beating you and allowing you to live like a – er . . . in a hotel back room.'

'That's a lie! Matt never beat me and the life I live is blameless.'

Brandon said nothing, but lifted his chin impassively.

She suddenly remembered the visit McAuley had paid her and the construction that might be put on it by the prurient – had been by Packham, the doughy-faced desk clerk. Though she knew she was innocent, a flush came to her cheeks. She wanted the interview with the stern doctor to be over, and terminated it as quickly as she could.

'I shall hire a buggy and go out to the ranch,' she said.

But her intention couldn't be fulfilled. At the livery barn, the proprietor correctly questioned

107

whether she could afford the rental, let alone a deposit.

'These are hard times, ma'am. I can't do no business with the Double H on a credit basis. Don't blame me fer that. You make your bed hard, you have to lie hard. Your husband is a known drunkard and now a cripple. Sure as shootin', he'll have consid-'rable difficulty payin' off his debts.'

In sinking spirits, she turned back to the hotel where she had her cheap and shabby quarters. A muddle of thoughts streamed through her head like flotsam on a dirty, storm-fed river.

Among the questions she had was why was Trinity Creek bad-mouthing herself and Matt every time it took the notion? Who'd put around the malicious story Matt had beaten her?

Delving back in her memory, she remembered how Alexander McAuley had first openly suggested she'd been abused by her husband, and how she'd hotly denied it. Could it be that he'd chosen to persist in his wrong thinking, maybe had stirred up the rabble who'd so grievously injured Matt?

The high-toned, low-moraled store proprietor was chief among the townsmen and an autocratic ruler of his businesses and his fine household. Ruthlessness and hypocrisy were in his nature. His manipulation of influence and money, plus support of the Unionist cause, had made him a prime political force and given him the confidence he could have anything he wanted. And she knew his wants included favours from herself she wasn't prepared to bestow.

With McAuley looming to the forefront of her mind, it came almost as no surprise to find the man himself waiting for her when she reached the hotel.

11

ALICE IN DANGER LAND

Alice was given no warning this time that a visitor had gained admission to her room. When she opened the door and saw Alexander McAuley, she tried to back out. Then she realized that was foolish. Her room was paid for her by Matt in advance on a weekly basis when he came to town. She had nowhere else she could go and little money of her own.

'Mr McAuley, you have no right to be here,' she said with all the force she could muster. 'Please will you leave?'

McAuley only smiled. 'On the contrary, Mr Burns, the hotelier, is a good friend. Moreover, I hold a mortgage on the real estate and have certain – uh – rights, which Mr Burns is happy for me to exercise.'

Alice took off the gloves she'd worn to visit the doctor and threw them down on the scratched and rickety dresser as though in a challenge.

'What do you want this time?'

'As always, to help you, my dear. I even bring you a small gift as a token of my esteem.'

He produced with a flourish a tortoise-shell music box. 'The latest thing in stock at the store from New Orleans. It plays ten tunes. Shall I demonstrate?'

She stamped her foot. 'I don't want your gewgaws, Mr McAuley, or anything else you care to offer!'

He tutted and tucked the rejected offering back in his coat pocket.

'Temper, temper. . . . You shouldn't be so hasty. The time must surely be mighty close when you'll have need of – uh – generous friendship.'

'What does that mean?'

'Well, it's no secret Harrison is laid up at the Double H, a cripple and his financial affairs in a parlous state. Who'll pay the rent for your room?'

'I shall!'

'How?'

'I— I'll work. I can teach again. In a *public* school.'

McAuley shook his head smugly. 'I think not. The county now has a board of examiners appointed to administer teachers' examinations under oath to the district judge. You won't pass your examination if you prove deficient in any particular. And I should mention, both the judge and the examiners are my good political friends. The only place you'll teach school will be a private home, such as my own.'

Alice was incensed at his arrogance and the injustice he implied.

'Why, that's abominable! You fiend!'

111

He laughed. 'Harsh names serve no purpose, pretty lady. You have to understand Harrison is washed up, finished. Howsoever, were you to be of a mind to make me happy – to consent to serve me in whatever outward capacity satisfies the conventions – your problems would be over. You'd have security.'

The unbelievably despicable, half-formed theories that had been lurking in the recesses of her mind burst from her lips in a torrent of words.

'How dare you press your suit yet again, Alexander McAuley! I hate you and do believe you were implicated in my husband's injuries.'

McAuley went white at the gills.

'Imagination, Mrs Harrison!' he jerked. 'Hokum . . . hysteria!'

She forged on, the dreadful truth becoming plainer to her as she gave it expression.

'I suspect you paid the mob that attacked Matt and your only regret is they didn't achieve his demise. I contemplate notifying the authorities. I shall make enquiries and, if appropriate, charge you with conspiring to murder my husband. I suggest you leave my room forthwith, or I'll scream this house down, and to hell with the scandal!'

To her satisfaction, and immense relief, he beat a prompt retreat under threat of the more dramatic dismissal. But he went muttering affronts.

McAuley repaired to the upstairs office back of his downtown emporium to assess his position. The comforting, subdued hum of money-making business went on below. Flour, best quality at fourteen dollars; second quality ten; sugar, twenty cents; coffee twenty-five per pound; bacon, twelve and fifteen per pound. . . . With the post-war prices of basic provisions so high, business wasn't brisk, but equally he was in a dominant trading position and couldn't go wrong.

The old office was familiar and snug and gave him reassurance. Here, he'd hatched many of the schemes that had made him a man of substance and a leading citizen of Trinity Creek. He filled and fired up a German pipe, sucking deeply on the curved stem and sinking deeply into the padded swivel chair behind the massive desk.

He was gravely concerned by Alice's closeness to the truth. Not for the first time, he cursed the incompetence of the thugs he'd paid to put an end to Matt Harrison. It was a pity Alice was no less intelligent than she was pretty. Measures would have to be taken to protect his interests before she began speaking out publicly.

Some of the mud she could throw – possibly the charges themselves – would stick, and he'd be destroyed, utterly.

Desirable though Alice Harrison's nicely blooming body might be, he couldn't risk his fortunes or his life to obtain such a prize, however thrilling and delightful it would have been to disrobe it, item by item, and take his pleasure.

After careful consideration and the jettisoning of long-held, cherished dreams, he ground out, talking to himself, 'I'll settle the bitch's hash yet. This way, she'll disappear from Texas completely.'

He would need help to carry out his scheme, but he had the contacts, and reckoned the hotel clerk, Packham, would be more than willing to put it quietly in train for a suitable, inexpensive sum of money.

Alice descended the threadbare-carpeted stairs knowing intuitively that trouble was lying in wait for her outside the musty confines of the hotel room that served as her only refuge.

But it was the familiar, leering clerk Packham who waylaid her when she reached the lobby.

'Oh, Mrs Harrison!' he called. 'A moment, please.' A glint was in his beady eyes and he seemed keyed-up in a pleasurable manner, like a cat contemplating play with a mouse.

'Yes? What is it?' she asked hollowly.

Packham coughed mildly and covered his mouth with his hand.

'Mr Burns has asked me to remind you that Mr Harrison hasn't come by to pay your room rent. He wants you to leave – today!'

'Why, that's impossible!' Alice responded, flabbergasted. 'Mr Burns must know my husband is presently incapacitated and unable to visit town. He's in bed and mending, Doc Brandon tells me. Mr Burns must wait, mustn't he?'

Packham shook his head regretfully. 'Now that wouldn't be very smart. The bill has to be paid. If Mr Burns listened to every hard-luck story he would soon be putting up the shutters and getting out of business.'

More politely, Alice said, 'I'm afraid I don't understand. Matt has always paid in advance. Surely we can be trusted.'

In her heart, she did understand. Using his influence, Alexander McAuley had struck like he'd said he would!

Again, the pimply clerk shook his head, this time with a smile tugging at his fat lips.

'You can take it from me that is the position.' He paused and made a show of reflection. 'Howsomever, I do believe I could put you on the track of alternative accommodation.'

'You could?' Alice was too distracted to disguise her eagerness.

'Yes, nothing as grand as a hotel room, I'm afraid,' Packham purred. 'Just a wooden shack at the town limits that might offer temporary shelter for a few dollars weekly. The owner is an absentee but he does make occasional visits and he'll be there tonight, after dusk. You'll have to speak to him. Come to an arrangement. He's a Mr Waldrop ... Woodson Waldrop is the full name, I believe.'

Expediency overrode Alice's more natural caution and she took the directions Packham gave her gratefully. The war over, everybody had been at a loss to know what to do for a living and a few householders had grabbed the chance to take Federal soldiers and officers to board. But the surly town was unlikely to offer her this alternative. Temporarily, she would perhaps prefer to rough it independently in this Mr Waldrop's shack, if it was possible.

That evening, it was darker than she would have

115

liked when she put on her cloak and slipped out of the township, leaving by a devious route that didn't bring her under the disapproving gaze of its citizens.

It was near full dark when she located the dilapidated wooden shack on the town's outskirts. Despite the inky-black shadows of some sheltering cottonwoods, she could see it was a hovel and unease stirred.

'Beggars can't be choosers,' she told herself, pulling her cloak closer and shivering.

Three horses stood patiently, hitched to a rail half-hidden at the back of the small building. One horse stamped and blew. Funny, she wouldn't have expected the shack's owner to have come with a small string. Light spilled from the cracks round the door and between the rips in a tattered window blind. She was going forward to tap on the door when a sudden apprehension of danger seized her.

She stopped, turned and was about to flee back to the roadway, when the door was shoved open and a shaft of yellow lamplight streamed out, melting the shadows and revealing her.

'Figgered I heard a lurkin' out thar,' a voice growled. 'Why don't yuh step on up, missy, 'stead o' slinkin' around in the dark? Me an' Rube'll be right glad to git acquainted.'

Alice gulped. 'Mr Waldrop? I think I've changed my mind. S-sorry! I'll be getting along now, back to town.'

'Hey! Hold up, gal—'

But Alice was running down the road. She hadn't liked one little bit the look of the man with the

116

hooked nose, the long sideburns and fringe of beard.

For a few moments, she thought they'd let her go, then she heard the hoofbeats above her panting breaths. The horses were ridden at no more than a gentle canter, but it was enough for them to catch up with her in no time flat.

'Dab it on 'er, Woody!' someone yelled.

Suddenly, a wide noose of spinning rope fell over her head, slid down and pinioned her arms to her slim waist. She was jerked to a sharp halt that flung her to the hard ground.

She heard coarse laughter. Soon as she got her breath, she began screaming for help. But she was still too far from town for anyone to hear.

12

GETTING TO THE TRUTH

'We've only your word for it, Jim,' Lena-Marie said, turning her head to him on the pillow. 'And we know you've been trying to blacken Woody Waldrop since the day you arrived. It's tiresome. Why not let it drop?'

Jim Hunter sighed. He had a feeling he was to be diverted – again.

She pulled him temptingly on top of her, but also closed her legs so he couldn't proceed to the next logical step in their lovemaking on her soft bed.

'Let's do other things than worry about shootings and intrigues. Bloodshed has always been general in these parts. The odd murder and attempted drygulching isn't so striking. One grows accustomed to it all and ceases to get excited about events of the petty criminal kind. Besides, a woman finds it hard to

118

work up interest in somebody else's fight. Even a man's she loves. . . .'

'All right then,' he said hoarsely as her witchery worked on him, taking his mind off everything but the demands and the skin-to-skin contact of the moment. 'Open your legs and lift up.'

She did.

The day he was ambushed in the sheepmen's country, Jim Hunter had returned to Palmito determined to lock horns with Woody Waldrop. But once more it was the Baptistes who held him back, telling him he had no proof of the gang leader's involvement – in the death of Walt Burridge, the disappearance of Tomas Vasquez, or this latest bushwhacking incident which Jim saw as an informed attempt on his own life.

It was hard not to believe the Baptistes, either Lena-Marie or Raoul, had deliberately or inadvertently tipped off Waldrop about Vasquez's story and brought his own subsequent movements under watch.

What other construction could be put on the facts as he knew them? That was the plumb truth of it anybody but a damned fool would acknowledge.

But the magic of Lena-Marie's beauty – the sheer physical allure of her – still held him to her. He just couldn't finish with her, walk out in defiance and face down Waldrop.

It was impossible for Jim to gather evidence of the wartime massacre by Waldrop of the Confederate patrol. At this late date, with the war receding into the past, did any exist? Without Tomas's face-to-face testimony, and with no way to prove Waldrop's guilt in the Mexican's disappearance, he couldn't see how he was to convince the beautiful Lena-Marie, who'd loved and protected him in both war and peace.

Nor did he fancy resuming his search for the Mexican boy who'd delivered the fake message. Riding out alone into back country would be like asking for a bullet in the back. He didn't think the men who wanted him dead would bungle a second chance to nail him.

But the matter of abducted Anglo women being traded into slavery was another matter. According to Tomas, this was current and might therefore be demonstrable.

When the idea occurred to him, Jim tingled at the promise in it and began to pry, carefully. The results were disappointing. Strange women guests were frequently booked into rooms at Palmito's single dowdy hotel, but they didn't leave their rooms during their apparently short stays and it was impossible for him to visit with them or monitor the circumstances of their comings and goings.

One night in the saloon, he observed a quick but meaningful exchange of looks between Raoul Baptiste and Woody Waldrop. Within minutes, both men had downed their drinks, bade goodnights to their respective groups of companions and strolled out through the batwings.

Jim quickly slipped out, too, and ghosted after their shadowy figures. They headed for the hotel and directed their furtive steps not to the front entrance but back of the premises to a more private door.

As the door opened and dim light spilled out from within, Jim melted swiftly into the black shadow of a veranda. Baptiste and Waldrop went inside and the door closed behind them. In moments, a thin outline of lamplight sprang into being around the pulled blind of a window adjacent to the door.

Jim glided across to the window and crouched beneath its sill, but it was closed and he could hear only an incomprehensible murmur of conversation.

He glanced swiftly right and left along the darkened back lots. Stealthily, he rose and went to the door. He found it unlatched and a gentle push opened it with the merest creak of hinges.

Inside was a short, uncarpeted passage lighted by an oil lamp standing on a small, bare table against one wall. A kitchen, dark except for the glow from a cooling woodstove, was to one side of the passage. To the other, a few paces along, the door to a lighted office stood ajar. Through it was coming Waldrop's voice. Raoul Baptiste was interjecting.

'It's a mighty dangerous game, holding these women here.'

Jim crept forward and halted rigid and motionless. Every word now came plainly to his ears.

'Ain't never been no trouble, Raoul,' Waldrop said, a mite aggravated. 'They're drugged an' it's dark when we bring 'em in an' take 'em out to the boats. Most always we keep 'em chained to the bed iron an' gagged.'

'And what if one should die while we wait for the next ship to call?'

Waldrop sniggered. 'That would be a pity. Some

fine womanflesh an' big dollars lost. Not to speak of the fun me an' the boys treat our ownselfs to meantime. But we could take care o' it. Like we did the Mex you tipped us off was gonna squeal to you an' your sister.'

'Women are trouble, Woody. Rape leads to lynchings. Always remember – even here where there's no law, it's playing with fire to mess with a woman.'

'Mebbe so,' Waldrop said with a lascivious chuckle. 'The one we got in chains upstairs right now sure is a *hot* piece of goods!'

Raoul took a deep, audible breath. 'Yeah . . . well, have your pleasure, but don't damage the merchandise or let any accident happen.'

'Only accident is liable to be that snoopy skunk Jim Hunter. He's still sniffin' around, yuh know.'

'Don't fret about him. Lena-Marie keeps him occupied plenty. She's got him under her thumb.'

Waldrop sniggered again. 'Only her thumb? I jest hope she don't believe anythin' he uncovers an' tells her. That's what it'd take to cook our goose, I reckon.'

'She trusts me, Woody. She don't listen to his unproven stories. Tread softly and we can keep it that way. Now I've got to go. . . . Hold in mind what I've said.'

Jim heard the faint scrape of a chair as though someone had pushed it back in rising. What he'd overheard had thrown his thoughts into an excited spin, but he wasn't so stunned by what he'd learned in the space of a few minutes not to know it would be useless information if he was caught. Quick as light, he scooted out of the hotel and behind one of the dark piles of trash accumulated back of Palmito's main-street buildings.

Nevertheless, he had the misfortune to be seen by one of Woody Waldrop's gang, Reuben Rasmussen. He was fading silently through an alley that would take him back to the front of the buildings when Rube turned into it at the far end. He lengthened his stride, thinking to brazen it out openly. But Rube wasn't fooled.

'Hunter! What're you doin' sneakin' 'round here? Where've you bin?'

'None of your business, Rube,' Jim said succinctly, knowing he was up against an astute, low-life hard-case and it wouldn't be enough.

Arrogantly, Rube made a grab for him as they drew level. 'That ain't—'

Jim was ready and Rube never got to finish. Jim flung himself aside, eluding Rube's hands, but fixing his own on the outlaw's throat.

Rube went to shout, but Jim's tightening grip turned it to a stifled rattle.

Jim realized that if he was caught in this place, coming clandestinely from the hotel where Waldrop and Baptiste had been conferring, the game would be up for him. He'd never be allowed the chance to unmask Raoul Baptiste and avenge the murders of Walt Burridge, Tomas Vasquez and countless others by Waldrop and his bunch.

He tightened his grip on Rube's neck, squeezing, crushing, working in his rigid thumbs. He summoned all his strength, reminding himself of how he'd escaped death by the narrowest of margins in a cunningly devised Waldrop ambush. He felt no compunction about what he was doing. He made himself believe the notion that he had the whole rotten gang in the retributive grip of his bare hands and was strangling them *en masse.*

Rube struggled and kicked and plucked and clawed at the backs of Jim's iron hands. With a thud, they toppled and rolled in the dirt.

Through it all, Jim maintained his pressure, enduring the minor hurts inflicted by his challenger. He couldn't afford to lose his advantage. From the outset, it had plainly been his life or Rube's. A fight to the death. The pity for Rube, and the luck for Jim, was that Rube hadn't known it and had been too confident of his own position.

Rube's face congested and his eyes bulged. Finally, after what seemed an age, he went limp with a blood-chilling gurgle. Still wary of a trick, Jim held on another full, eerie, silent minute.

At last, he relaxed his grip and felt for a heartbeat. There was none.

Jim got up and straightened up, cursing the complication introduced by the Waldrop adherent's death into a situation he'd not yet figured out how to handle. In less than a half-hour, the affair had erupted into crisis upon crisis.

First off, he had to hide Rube Rasmussen's uglily throttled corpse, at least temporarily. He dragged it back down the alley, away from the main street, then along to the back of a derelict warehouse where an optimistic German immigrant had set up a fish processing and packing business before the war. He dragged it under a loading platform and surrounded it with foul-smelling sacks of trash from the back lots.

That was the practical, easy part.

Not so readily resolved was how to tackle the Baptistes and Waldrop. Jim felt a great sorrow for Lena-Marie. Plainly from what he'd learned this night, she was not aware of the full extent of Waldrop's rackets or her brother's involvement.

From the main street, Jim looked up at the Palmito House. Lights shone in the rambling, two-storey hotel overlooking the main drag. At least one woman, earmarked for a life of enslavement, was held captive somewhere inside that building, being subjected to God knew what.

Lena-Marie's brother had turned a blind eye to this — among other heinous crimes, like dooming Tomas Vasquez to death by tipping off Waldrop he was going to spill the beans on his, Waldrop's, wartime conduct.

Lena-Marie would be devastated, Jim knew. Though she loved Raoul, she followed a code of honour. His exposure would have to result in their alienation.

Jim sat on the steps to a boardwalk and addressed his problem silently to the drift of winking stars that sprinkled the vast blackness of the heavens above him. It offered no comment on the infamy of puny, mortal men.

Maybe because of his own split with Matt, whom he'd regarded as a brother, Jim was troubled. He figured from his personal experience that Lena-

Marie and Raoul's break-up under much more shameful circumstances would cause her great pain. Yet Lena-Marie was not a bad woman at bottom. She didn't deserve the heartbreak.

A sudden gust of onshore breeze brought a powerful smell of ozone, of kelp and wet nets into the township. And on the breeze came an answer.

13

'QUIT TOWN OR DIE!'

In the back room of the Gulf Trader the night was eerily, uncommonly still. At the open window, the flimsy blind tapped listlessly from time to time in a vagrant sea breeze. The voices of patrons in the bar-room produced only a low buzz. At this late hour, no one played the piano; Lena-Marie wasn't singing.

Raoul Baptiste, alone with his thoughts, was conscious of a certain disquiet after his meeting with Woody Waldrop. He watched a long black cigarette burn away in an ashtray. He wondered if he shouldn't have persuaded the gang leader to return with him to the office to share a convivial bottle of whiskey privately.

He was reflecting a quiet session here might have

kept the man out of more dangerous mischief else-where when the locked door was rapped demand-ingly.

Startled, he asked, 'Who is it?'

'Jim Hunter. Open up!'

His response came harshly. 'Why the hell do I need to see you at this godawful hour, Hunter?'

'Because I say so!' The words that blurted out of Lena-Marie's latest dupe were driven by terrible anger. 'You'd better open this door straightaway, less'n you want me to kick it in and blow your head clean off your shoulders!'

Jim Hunter noted with a grim satisfaction that Baptiste started in fear when he saw the drawn Colt in his right fist.

'Don't wet your fancy pants,' Jim said, and there was contempt in his voice as he thought of the misery Lena-Marie's evil and undeserved brother had condoned. 'I ain't going to kill you – not yet. . . .'

Baptiste's hand hovered as if he was about to reach for the drawer of his desk where he and his sister kept an old Allen derringer. But he thought better of it. The revolver in Jim's hand was steady as a rock.

'What do you want, Hunter? Are you drunk? Have you taken leave of your senses?'

Jim felt a thrill of excitement at the man's shock. At last he was coming to grips with the rottenness in Palmito. For weeks he'd hunted for the leads that would tell him what was really going on in the Gulf village and enable him to destroy Woodson Waldrop and all he stood for. Tonight everything had fallen into place. Vengeance was soon to be his!

'No, I ain't drunk. Nor crazy. This is the end of the line in Palmito for you, Raoul Baptiste. I know about the kidnappings and killings and the rest. To get to the point, your stinking outfit's finished!'

Baptiste tried bluff, assuming a false bonhomie.

'Jim, friend! That isn't your ownself talking – your life is here now, with Lena-Marie and me. We need you. Stay with us and together we'll take over all the coastal lands! The Baptistes are out for wealth and power, and I don't give a damn how we get it. Shooting, smuggling whores . . . anything to secure what we want!'

'No, Raoul!' Jim snapped. 'I'm winding up your operation, then I'm starting over with a clean slate. But to spare your sister distress, and in consideration of her being largely innocent of the despicable crimes you've carried out with Waldrop, I'm giving you a chance.'

At his mention of a reprieve, Baptiste regained a measure of confidence.

'A chance – pah! You don't know what you're going up against, cowboy. You can't kill me here and now anyway. You do and you'll be dead before you can ride out of Texas. Lena-Marie will order it herself, however handsomely you perform in her bed.'

Jim began to wonder if the concession he planned to offer was wise.

'Shut your dirty mouth, Baptiste! Listen up good.

You've admitted you know about the abductions and shipping of good American women. And Waldrop's the mad-dog killer I always said he was. I aim to fix him—'

'You're dreaming!' Baptiste interjected.

'But I want peace for your sister – for the whole territory – by cleaning out vicious gangs like yours and Waldrop's. In exchange for your life and telling Lena-Marie nothing of your deviancy, I want your word you'll break up the gang and quit town by noon tomorrow.'

Raoul Baptiste laughed scornfully, gaining courage from the melodramatic absurdity of Jim's immature idealism.

'I'll give no such thing, saddle-tramp! I'm still the master here; you're just another hired hand. You'll keep away from my sister and Waldrop and the boys. And you'll be the one to quit town, or die!'

Jim was jarred by Baptiste's recovery. Something like amusement was on the crook's smooth Latin features.

'You reckon, huh?'

'I do. You don't seem to recall my reputation as a gunfighter. Let me give *you* an ultimatum: if I see you on Main Street at noon, it'll be to kill you!'

Jim swore softly, angrily, hearing the thudding beat of his own heart.

'We'll see about that.'

Matt Harrison seethed with rage and anxiety in the lobby of Burns's hotel in Trinity Creek. It was the first time he'd made it to town since his injury by the mob. He'd consumed a large quantity of cheap, redeye liquor on the journey to deaden the pain from his legs. But the mighty effort had sharpened his feelings.

'How do you mean, there isn't any rent to pay?' he thundered at the clerk. 'My wife can't pay it herself. So what goes on up there?'

Packham swallowed. 'Sh-she isn't – er – available, sir. Isn't here any more.'

'Don't give me that! She's got no place else to go. I want to see her.'

Disbelieving, swinging on his gimpy legs, Matt made for the stairs, unaided and uninvited. He hauled himself up using the handrail. The balustrades creaked and shifted alarmingly.

Packham bleated incoherently but made no attempt to stop him. He was doubtless glad to see Matt's back, however briefly.

Matt was incensed. Crippled, wobbly on his feet, he maintained a muscular torso, powerful arms and big fists, while Packham was a poor specimen of manhood. The hardest work he did in his unhealthy life was entering the correct figures in hotelier Burns's ledgers. Packham was good at doing sums. He hadn't the imagination for much else, but he did have enough to picture the mess a riled Matt Harrison could make of his puffy face and body.

Since the war, his marriage and subsequent events, the Double H rancher had been a changed man from the equable character he'd been before. Some said liquor and his beating had played the final part in his metamorphosis.

Matt's wrath mounted with every rise of the stairs. Breathing hard, he reached the top and lurched along the narrow upper hallway, bouncing off the walls till he reached the last door on the right.

He flung it open violently, so the inner knob made a deep impression in the wall and the door swung back violently. He met it with his broad shoulder and burst in.

Empty! The bed was unmade: no sheets, no blankets, just a stained mattress. Matt pulled open the drawers of the scarred dresser. Nothing. None of the little, private things that would have told him Alice had ever been here.

Like a wild man, he plunged back down the stairs to confront the quivering clerk.

Packham recoiled from Matt's cold, basilisk stare as though he'd been hit in the face. Sweat broke out on his pimply forehead. If he'd ever seen death in a man's eyes, he saw it now.

'She's gone,' Matt said with drunken deliberation.

'T-told you, sir. Not here any more.'

Matt seized Packham by the shirtfront, bunching it in his fist. With the brute strength in his right arm, he dragged the misshapen clerk forward till his round, protuberant belly fought for space with the register on the desk top. An ink well was sent flying, spattering both men before rolling across the floor, trailing a blue-black arc.

'I'm not halfway satisfied with your answers, kid,' Matt said, grim-faced and implacable. 'You want I should beat the truth out of you?'

132

Packham was brought eyeball-to eyeball with Matt, so close he could hear the grinding of his teeth and smell the whiskey as he spat out his anger. A scare was well and truly thrown into him.

'N-no! Please! They say she's left town. Emigrated. . . .'

'*What. . . !*'

'It was Mr – Mr McAuley's idea. None o' mine. He paid up the debt with Burns. He's a great one for plots and schemes is Mr McAuley. Everyone knows that! He handled it all hisself. Really, I didn't do a thing!'

Matt eased his hold a little.

'No, you haven't got the balls,' he said, deciding he'd prised as much out of Packham as was possible. 'In point of fact, you've prob'ly got nothing there bigger'n the pimples on your ugly mug.'

Then his pain and anger reasserted themselves. He clenched his left hand in a fist and drove it into Packham's slobbering face.

Packham was smashed back behind his desk in a heap, his nose and mouth bloody. Yellow pus oozed from ruptured spots. He shrieked.

'Oh, my God! I'm bleeding. You've broken my nose.'

Matt acted like he didn't hear him. Naked anguish was in his eyes. He was frantic. Where would he find Alice? How would he find Alice? The questions rang through his head like a shout.

Of course . . . the answer was through McAuley. That's where his staggering legs had to carry him now.

Young Packham was one of numerous townie no-accounts who lurked behind the Trinity Creek throne sat on by Alexander McAuley. Giving the miserable clerk no thanks for the information he'd extracted from him, Matt reeled out of the hotel and limped in the direction of McAuley's big house, every footstep a new and painful effort.

The easiest approach for a disabled man was via the schoolroom at the back of the house. Matt's preparations for his journey to town by buckboard had taken more time than he could afford. It was now late in the day, school was out and McAuley's brats were playing in the backyard. They tittered as the lamed man, the worse for spiritous drink, hobbled into their classroom, but they made no move to help or hinder him.

'Pa's with Miss Smith,' the eldest called. '*Private*. They'll be plumb ratty if you shove in on 'em.'

Matt ignored them. He lumbered on from the small school into the home. It was a place of grandeur with stained timber panelling and thick carpet in the halls, but Matt gave notice to none of this.

He heard voices behind a door ahead of him. They belonged to McAuley and Miss Ruby Smith. He couldn't make out words, but he could the frivolous, teasing tones and the giggling. McAuley and his schoolmistress were engaged in intercourse of a kind that had nothing to do with any educational curriculum known to a moral world.

Seeing red, he threw the door wide unceremoniously.

The parlour room was furnished in expensive dark woods, accented with genuine crystal lamps and silky crimson drapes. Again, none of this Matt noticed.

Ruby was seated on a heavy, high-backed chair with velvet-upholstered arms and back. She was *en déshabillé* and had her white legs hooked over the arms. McAuley was on his knees before her, between dangling feet which Matt somehow noticed had red-painted toenails.

Ruby screamed and McAuley turned and jumped up.

'I trust I am interrupting something,' Matt said scathingly.

'This is an outrage!' McAuley roared. 'It's indecent. Get out!'

But Matt wasn't interested in arguing about his insult to the privacy of their entertainment. He went straight to his business.

'The hell with decencies you've already offended! I figure you know why I'm here. I stay till you tell me what you've done with my wife, you skunk!'

'Don't know what you're talking about!' McAuley said, red-faced.

Meanwhile, Ruby made what Matt supposed was a move to remedy her disgraceful state of undress. She lifted her legs free of the chair arms and reached down for the discarded garments close by her on the floor. But what she actually did was snatch a small pistol from its hiding place in a specially sewn stocking top.

Ruby, it was confirmed, was one of those 'ladies of

the night' who'd learned in her Western wanderings it was advisable for a vulnerable woman to carry a deadly weapon for the defence of what scrap might be left of her honour.

The gun was a tiny Remington Vest Pocket .22. But Ruby balked at shooting the intruder with her own trembling hand. She thrust it into McAuley's hand.

'Take the gun! Quick – kill the bastard!'

The Remington was of one thousands of small pistols of its kind that had gone West with emigrants and gold rushers. Such guns saw service in many a booming town – in gambling squabbles, duels, assassinations and bordello brawls. They could be bought for a mere ten dollars compared to upward of twenty-five for a workmanlike Colt such as Matt had at his hip.

But McAuley had not done active service in the war. He was a storekeeper who'd progressed to businessman. He had next to no experience with the use of a firearm. He fumbled with the pistol.

Matt saw the Remington pass between them. His vision was blurry and his judgement impaired by the medicine he'd chosen for his cares and injuries. What he knew for sure was that a gun had been produced, the stakes had been upped and his own life was at risk.

Thus a horrifying tragedy unfolded.

In high excitement, Ruby screamed, 'Shoot, Alex, shoot!'

As McAuley raised the pistol to fire point-blank, Matt smoothly whipped his Colt from its holster. Two shots crashed deafeningly in the confines of the parlour.

Matt's was the first by a split-second and the slug struck McAuley over the nose, exiting from the crown of his head in a fountain of blood, bone and grey matter. He was instantly hurled off his feet and into oblivion.

The Remington discharged possibly as McAuley's finger tightened reflexively, finally, on the trigger. The impact of the Colt's bullet was already throwing him backwards and sideways and with the little hide-out gun falling from its mark and swinging, its shot could only go wild.

Unforeseeably, unstoppably, the Remington's .22 slug made a hole in Ruby's bare abdomen. It lodged inside her but wasn't immediately fatal.

She didn't realize the hurt was critical. She said to Matt, who still fisted his smoking gun at the ready, 'Please don't kill me! I didn't mean no harm. McAuley's dead. You better get outa here fast.'

Matt was jerked into sobriety by the enormity and destruction of the shooting. He'd seen many men gut-shot in the war and knew Ruby was mortally wounded. For several moments, she seemed to be unaware of it, but then abruptly she went as white as a sheet. With a weak cry, she fainted.

Matt wiped the forearm of his shirt across his sweating forehead. The loud reverberations of the shots had left a thousand hammers at work inside his skull. He was unnerved. Everything had gone to pieces too suddenly for a mind that had been mired in the murk of anger, pain and liquor.

In panic, he ran from the room and the dying

woman, knowing that McAuley and Ruby's blood was on his hands. All he could think to do was get back to the buckboard and ride out fast for the safety of the Double H.

Run to earth. Hole up.

14

A DREAM OF DEATH

Jim Hunter didn't entirely trust Raoul Baptiste not to pass word to Woody Waldrop that he was going to eliminate him in a spectacular noon shootout. Raoul didn't lack for courage or pride, and he had a full measure of vanity, but Jim's fear was that if it was put around in advance he'd lost the protection of the Baptistes' favour, his life would be in immediate jeopardy from Waldrop and his low-principled riff-raff.

He could see only one way to gain some needed sleep, and that was in Lena-Marie's bed, which she was always willing to share with him.

But, of course, although he was safe at her side, the notion he could rest proved a delusion. It was the first occasion he didn't provide the sensuous Lena-Marie with a worthy partner.

'Something tells me your heart is not in this, Jim,'

she said as her exploring fingers failed to excite a response. 'In fact, I don't think you're here at all tonight.'

He bestowed a kiss that ignited no fire in his lips; tender, but passionless.

'Maybe you have a headache!' Lena-Marie said, trying to make light of it with a laugh. 'You want for vigour. Perhaps I should let you sleep a while. . . .'

'Yeah,' Jim breathed. 'It could be for the best. If it's all right with you, I'd be much obliged.'

'My! So formal, so contrite. What's wrong, Jim?'

He dared not tell her. If Raoul didn't use the chance he'd given him to decamp, and persisted with his declared intention to meet him in a gun duel at noon, she was going to lose a brother or a lover. This would be the last time he came to her bed, and he'd come to it for a passel of wrong reasons. Where their relationship was concerned, he would be on a high-way to nowhere.

She could never be his again.

'Nothing,' he lied guiltily. 'Just tired.'

Somewhere in the distance dogs were disturbed and barked, and constantly, monotonously in the background was the sound of waves breaking on the Gulf shore. . . .

They turned on their sides, pulled up the sheets and tried to sleep.

Incredibly, Jim did. And dreamed, though it had the quality of the worst nightmare.

He and Lena-Marie had fled to Mexico and were in an ornately appointed Spanish mission with rich tapestry hangings and golden statuary. They were at their wedding ceremony. The brown-robed priest marrying them was breathlessly excited and repeatedly touched Lena-Marie in grotesquely inappropriate ways.

The scene switched abruptly to a bed-chamber into which the same priest had eagerly intruded.

'My children,' the priest said, 'why are you not ready for me? For it is my duty, according to Spanish law and the Holy Order's rites, to see your marriage consummated. I have your signed bond promising to perform the act before me, and I must take the stained bedsheets as evidence it has been done.'

The scene switched to a plaza under an ominously stormy sky where the priest was holding up for the approval of a cheering crowd not sheets, but Lena-Marie's white wedding gown.

Oddly, the priest's face melted into the hook-nosed profile and malevolent features of Woody Waldrop, but the transformation didn't seem strange, only frightening.

The garment the robed man flourished was holed in the bodice and from there down was drenched darkly red with blood.

Jim was woken by his own distressed, choking cry of protest.

Alice Harrison was cut off from all communication with the outer world. She was chained wrist and ankle to a bed in an upstairs room in what she thought must be a hotel or boarding-house of a sort more run-down and squalid than that she'd occupied in Trinity Creek.

141

Through a dirty window, she could glimpse the sky. Tonight it was changing. As the hours of darkness dragged, clouds built steadily. She thought a storm might be on its way.

Somewhere in the distance dogs were disturbed and barked, and constantly, monotonously in the background was the sound of waves breaking on a sea-shore. . . .

She'd lost count of the days of her captivity, yet she had a premonition events were coming to a head. If the approaching climax was not a storm but her death, so be it. She'd latterly endured all the depravity that could be visited on a woman. Death would be a merciful release.

At first, they'd kept her gagged as well as chained, but she'd quickly learned it was best for her not to holler for help. Then, Waldrop or one or other of his henchmen would quickly appear. She'd be punched and thrashed brutally, often with their leather belts, back or front. When she was reduced to unresisting sobs, they'd do the other things to her that she'd once always supposed – and experienced as – pleasures. Now she knew they could be the most degrading and painful torture.

Since Waldrop forced her spitefully and daily, sometimes more, she chose not to invite the extra abuse, fearing disease or permanent injury. She kept quiet and was left ungagged.

Exhaustion and malnutrition had their effect and she dozed, then slept deeply.

She woke long after morning had broken. Clouds were rolling over her patch of sky at all altitudes in what she figured, going by repeated past observation of the passage of the sun, was from a north-easterly direction.

Despite the absence of the sun now, she also calculated it was one of the times she could expect a visit from Waldrop. Her insides cringed and her wrists tugged involuntarily at their shackles. She moaned at the anticipated horror of his loathsome attentions.

The thought of it seemed to summon the reality. Within moments, Waldrop arrived in the sparsely furnished room with an ugly smile on his lips under the hooked nose and above the fringe of beard. Triumph? Mockery? Hunger?

This time, she felt, was going to be different. He was more than usually keyed-up. And he carried a gun; a long gun like the breechloading Henry repeating rifle that Matt had brought back from the war and said had far more fire power than any other firearm available.

'Howdy, slut,' Waldrop said. 'Time to pay fer your board! Make up your mind to do it without a struggle an' I'll unloose yuh from the chains fer a change. Whadyuh say to that?'

Resistance was futile. Alice licked her dry lips and nodded. 'If you say so. Just let me have some water first.'

Waldrop jeered, 'I like a woman that's easy pleased.'

He propped the rifle against the wall by the window and gave her the water, spilling much of it from the cracked cup over her chin. He freed her of the cruel weight of the chains, and she sighed.

'Haw!' he said, reading her reaction wrongly,

though surely deliberately, sarcastically. 'Yuh'll enjoy it today, slut. It'll be hot an' sweet – 'magine that! But no squealin', mind. . . .'

Though she was unrestrained, the next few minutes were no less an ordeal for Alice than they'd ever been. She felt physically sickened by how she was used, the wet dirtying of her body. Before her kidnapping, she'd been a woman to whom even a kiss had seemed a sacred thing.

Outside, a rising wind slammed doors and rattled shutters. The dogs began their barking.

To her surprise, Waldrop's grunts as he had his way with her suggested he didn't exact as complete a relish from the attack – she could give it no exculpating name – than he had from earlier exercises of his lust. Every time, it was rape.

When he'd got through with her, he pulled up and rebuttoned his pants, careless of the gross rudeness she momentarily saw of him, and with his mind plainly elsewhere. He didn't replace his gunbelt with its twin holstered revolvers.

To Alice, he appeared to give no further thought to her. She was something he'd used up for the moment. She was done: exhausted, prostrated, left soiled and limp, without strength or will to give him trouble. He didn't bother to reattach her to the iron frame of the hard, fusty bed with the chains.

Preoccupied, he raised the window sash, which screeched drily in its warped frame. He stationed himself to one side of it and took up the rifle.

Jim Hunter stayed in Lena-Marie's room till well after

144

he'd heard Palmito's clocks strike eleven. He noted with a distracted part of his troubled mind that the wind was rising.

From the window, he saw the thickening rain clouds. The Gulf had had little cloud cover for several weeks, the air had been relatively still and the seas had been as warm and almost as calm as bathwater. Today, he heard the stranger sound of surf pounding on the beach, and warmth wasn't the word for what he felt or the storm brewing in his heart. He was chilled. Too, the remnants of his ugly dream of death lingered disturbingly in his mind and wouldn't be thrown off.

Craning his neck, he could see a coastal schooner, trim and graceful and anchored several hundred yards from the jetty, bobbing on the Gulf's swells. The frailer craft of the Mexican fishermen were also in a state of perpetual motion. No fishing would be done today or tonight if the weather continued to deteriorate.

He was filled with foreboding. Lena-Marie hadn't returned to her room since she'd risen at first light. Jim was sure she would have done if she'd discovered Raoul had hightailed it from Palmito during the night, or was making preparations to pull his freight any time soon.

He cleaned and reloaded his long-barrelled Colts. A few minutes before noon, he buckled his cartridge belt round his lean hips. It was time to go out there.

He left the room and made his way quietly by the back stairs to the rear entrance of the Gulf Trader. He looked out, feeling the lifting wind with its salt tang on his peering face, then slid through the doorway.

Whatever transpired in the next short while, Jim knew the effects would be lasting – not for just an hour, not for just a day, not for just a year, but always.

He was sure of Raoul Baptiste now. The Latin meant for them to meet on the main street at noon. For one of them, it would be the last play; his last stand.

Lena-Marie would also be a loser, regardless of the outcome. Maybe that had been the message of his bizarre nightmare, if it had one.

But at the time these thoughts came to him, Jim – like everyone else – had no real idea of just how fateful the clash was to be for Lena-Marie.

Nor of the scale of the disaster about to befall Palmito.

15

STORMY RECKONING

It was noon; the hour of reckoning. Jim Hunter squared his shoulders and moved into the very middle of the street. The main drag had been emptied, either by the weather or by a last-minute announcement by Raoul Baptiste to his associates of what was about to go down.

But Raoul was there in the open, as he'd promised, striding toward him in a determined, business-like manner. Dust devils skipped around his heels and swirled on the high wind.

His face held no emotion other than a sardonic contempt, a disbelief; he was confident in his gun skills.

The same wind that followed Raoul stung Jim's face and eyes with the same dust. He realized that, walking into the unexpected wind, he was at a disadvantage. He swore softly and the grit got into his mouth, between his tight-clenched teeth.

This was the showdown. The issue was to be decided not by what was right or wrong, fair or unfair, but by the gunspeed and accuracy of two men, each convinced that his was the only way forward.

Lena-Marie flung a brilliantly embroidered shawl across her shoulders and looked out over the batwings of the Gulf Trader. She was assessing the likelihood of heavy rain coinciding with high tide, and the possibility of a resulting flood in the seafront quarter, when she saw the two steadfastly converging figures. She gasped.

Sweet Jesus! The idiots were going to shoot out their differences!

She pulled close the shawl and rushed out on to the street, rashly determined to put a stop to the nonsense. The trouble, as she saw it, was not of a kind that some brilliant shooting would disperse. That way led only to loss. Effectively isolated though they might be from the law of the United States of America, the implications for her affections and interests were hateful.

Raoul was closest, his back to her, and Jim was striding down the street toward them. She was about to call Raoul's name when her eye was caught by a movement at an upstairs window of the ramshackle Palmito House behind Jim.

The barrel of a rifle had appeared and was being trained on Jim's back. He was walking into an ambush.

Her indignant call became instead an anguished scream of warning.

'*N-o-o . . . ! Behind you, Jim! Get off the street*!'

Simultaneously, the leaden skies let fall the first heavy drops of rain.

Alice continued to watch Woody Waldrop. His back was turned to her completely at the window of the squalid room that was her prison. Speculation replaced the hurt and loathing in her eyes.

Occasionally, as Waldrop fixed his attentive gaze on whatever scene lay below – probably, from the sounds she'd heard, a street in a small town with a large Mexican element – he would chuckle quietly to himself, as though he was anticipating the unfolding of a satisfying joke.

He was engrossed: staring, staring. . . . His using of her body was quite forgotten. *She* was quite forgotten.

Well, she could tell him now – but wouldn't – she was far from as spent and as docile as he'd assumed. His carelessness was uncustomary. It might not happen again. If ever she was to try to regain her freedom, now was the time.

She shifted her bruised and aching limbs tentatively. Whatever the horrors of Waldrop's latest bout with her, the shackles had been removed from her wrists and ankles, which had allowed her circulation to revive. She was able to move, albeit painfully and stiffly.

She sat up and edged her feet off the bed to the floor. Still he didn't notice and her boldness grew. She rose from the bed slowly, fearing it might give her away with a creak. But it had been chosen for stoutness and firmness, no doubt with the rigorous uses its occupants would be put to in mind.

Her eyes alighted on Waldrop's discarded gunbelt. Dare she? Yes, she had to. She crouched and eased a heavy Colt revolver from the greasy leather of its holster.

At the window, Waldrop was more intent on his unknown task than ever. He'd raised the rifle to his shoulder and was sighting along it.

Alice tiptoed up behind him on her bare feet. She had to incapacitate him somehow and get out, but she was intrigued to know the target that had taken his whole attention. Letting her glance fly beyond him to the street outside, she saw it was a man walking alone with his broad back to the hotel to meet another man advancing similarly from the street's other end.

Her heart flew into a thousand pieces and she nearly let loose an involuntary cry.

She knew the man targeted by Waldrop. It was her old beau and her husband's ex-partner, Jim Hunter!

A vivid red bandanna of the kind he admired to wear fluttered wildly. His high-crowned hat with the fancy band was tilted forward rakishly as always, tied firmly under his chin against the tug of the wind.

She couldn't see his honest face, but the loved and familiar figure created an image of it in her mind. As he went to meet the other man in obvious challenge, it would be set as she imagined it might be in death – without emotion, bleak, and with the cheek muscles ridged against the weather-tanned skin.

And Waldrop's crooked finger was tightening murderously on the trigger of the rifle pointed at his back.

'Ain't about to risk lettin' Hunter kill yuh, Raoul ol' pard!' he muttered.

Gone quite cold, but without a shiver and steady, Alice raised the revolver she held in both hands and trained it at Waldrop's head.

Outside, a woman in a bright, flying shawl ran up behind the man Waldrop had called Raoul and screamed. At the same time, the darkening skies opened up in a downpour.

Alice barely noticed these things. She was firing point-blank into the back of her tormentor's head. A committed assassin's head.

She'd parted her feet and braced her legs for the gun's recoil, but she staggered back, her insides and legs gone to jelly the instant she'd done what she'd had to.

Whatever vice-addled brains Waldrop possessed were blown out of his skull and out the window in a shower of blood and bone fragments.

Immediately, everything else went out the window, too.

The rifle swinging in his hands discharged with a vicious crack and a spurt of flame, sending its deadly load on its way she saw not where. Waldrop, dead as he fired, toppled through, taking glass and a splintered hunk of the frame with him.

Even then, to Alice, it seemed like there were four shots in all – two more distant, from the street. But the falling rain had become a sudden, teeming

151

deluge. Its rattle on the hotel roof made indistinct all but the closest sounds.

She did hear Waldrop's falling body make a booming crash below the window – possibly as it bounced off the tin of an awning – followed by a meaty thud as it hit ground.

Alice herself also fell, to the bare boards of the floor. She struggled against an onset of nauseous weakness to rise and establish the full results of her deadly action and what had happened on the street.

Nothing came soon enough to stop the commencement of Jim Hunter's and Raoul Baptiste's fight. Guns were to sing their fatal song above the howl of the coming storm.

Jim saw Lena-Marie run out into the roadway behind her brother but he was unaware of her presence. All his attention was on Raoul's hovering right hand as he went into a crouch.

Raoul's hand slapped down for his gun. Jim snatched for his.

Lena-Marie was suddenly letting out words in a terrified scream and rain was making big spatters.

Distracted by Lena-Marie's ear-splitting shriek of warning, Raoul sent the shot he fired into an awning support on the left of Jim and far wide. It sent splinters flying but did no other damage.

Jim was the steadier marksman. The shot from his gun, which blazed at almost the identical instant to Raoul's, took him squarely in the region of the heart.

Simultaneously, he heard a muffled report above and behind him succeeded by the unmistakable crack of a powerful rifle from the same direction. He flung himself to the roadway, ripping a knee out of his pants, fearing he'd been tricked and was about to be wiped out in a street-bracketing crossfire.

But the rifle spoke only once. And then, with an abrupt heaven-shattering roar, the mighty rushing wind of a hurricane hit the town and all was chaos, blurred by sweeping curtains of rain.

Jim turned to see a body and a rifle – possibly a Henry lever-action repeating rifle – lying in the street. Through the deluge the body looked already like a sack of wet meal, but he recognized it as Woody Waldrop.

Looking back in the opposite direction, a more horrific sight met his eyes. By an awful freak of chance, the bullet from the Henry rifle – it fired a .44 metallic cartridge – had struck Lena-Marie in the breast. She'd been knocked off her feet and thrown back several yards. In dreadful enactment of his dream, blood streamed down from the holed bodice of her gown.

The gay shawl was whipping away up the street on the wind.

Lena-Marie got on to all fours and crawled to her brother's side. Her black hair hung in wet strings and her clothes were saturated by rain. And blood.

She rose up on to her knees. Her blood stained the head she cradled in her arms. Quickly as the rain washed the red away in pink rivulets, more spurted darkly from her terrible wound. For the space of ten seemingly interminable seconds she hunched there, head bent, breath coming and going in harsh sobs.

Then she toppled across Raoul's body, choked on blood which erupted from her mouth and was still.

The rain kept falling in torrents.

Jim hurried to the huddled pair, saw there was nothing he could do for either, and darted for cover on the boardwalk outside the Gulf Trader.

He shook his wet head in disbelief and despair. A vast, aching emptiness took hold of his insides. He felt sick. Waldrop had probably meant to back-shoot him, but who had killed Waldrop?

'Goddamnit! This is one hell of a mess.'

Running feet slapped wetly behind him. He wheeled, his hand automatically going for his revolver, which he'd already returned to the holster. He was astonished to see a scantily clad, shoeless young woman. Moreover, the flimsy, drenched garments were pasted to a figure he instantly recognized.

'*Alice!*' he exclaimed. 'How – why. . . ?'

Explanations of the sketchiest kind were exchanged in the saloon. Clothes were found for Alice. Lena-Marie's girls were a hard lot, but gave their sympathy and help without asking, regardless of their own state of shock.

The place was shaking in the hurricane and the people sheltering there said they'd never known the like. The afternoon wore on, and still the rain fell and the high wind tore at the town. Only the fool-hardy and the most worried for loved ones and property elsewhere ventured out from the saloon.

As dusk came to Palmito, the few lights lit glinted

on a scene of devastation. More people arrived in dishevelled, wearied condition, reporting heavy damage.

'The town's drenched in death,' Jim and Alice were told.

Nobody expressed any interest in the fate of the Baptistes or Woody Waldrop. Their own lives were under threat.

The hurricane had brought with it a storm surge of more than fifteen feet. It had smashed the Mex quarter on the shore, washing over the 'dobes and shacks. The surf had pounded them and their contents to pieces.

The destructive waters lifted debris from one row of buildings and hurled it against the next row until eventually the entire quarter was flattened. People striving to make their way through wind and water to refuge were struck by hurtling flotsam.

One Mexican said he'd seen a woman decapitated by a flying slate from a roof.

From Lena-Marie's upstairs window, Jim observed in the last of the failing light that the jetty was gone, and the remains of the wrecked and once graceful schooner had been carried far inland. Only a wall of debris stood between the main part of town and the angry ocean.

'We should evacuate from this horrible place!' Alice said.

'We will, but it ain't possible yet,' Jim said.

Leaving a building meant death by drowning; staying courted death in its wreckage.

Between six and seven o'clock the wind became

almost due east and increased in violence. Wreckage fairly flew past in the flooded main street outside, and the tide was still rising, once leaping fully four feet in a single bound at what had once been the shoreline.

In a few minutes, several of the clapboard houses closest to the sea were engulfed and toppled from their foundations. Some of the pieces floated past the Gulf Trader on the muddy brown waters.

Many left the saloon in a vain bid to seek greater safety, but the waters rose to chest-deep and higher. The carpetbagger banker with the gold-rimmed spectacles who'd had such grand plans for the little town and its port tried to set out in a wagon heaped with chests presumably containing his wealth. The story came back that the wagon was capsized and the banker crushed or drowned in the wreck.

Jim and Alice retreated to the saloon's upper floor.

'Pray that the foundations are firm and the place doesn't get torn off them,' Jim said.

A bad night was had. Not until early next morning did the fury of wind and water abate, though the sea's swells continued and the skies stayed cloudy. Fully two-thirds of the town was gone. Corpses were washed up everywhere, though where those of the Baptistes and Woody Waldrop had drifted, Jim couldn't ascertain.

Not that he made an exhaustive search.

'It's over. It's all over. And we're among the few left,' he told Alice. 'Palmito is finished – wiped off the map. Maybe it's a good thing, too. The place had a rotten heart.'

Miraculously, the livery stable had survived the storm and the flooding. Jim got along there fast, ahead of others who might take the same notion. He saddled up his chestnut and commandeered an ageing but sound grey for Alice. The one-armed hostler was nowhere in evidence. Either he'd high-tailed it from the town early or he'd been one of the hurricane's scores of casualties.

Alice said, 'I want to go back to Trinity Creek – to Matt, and to do something about Alexander McAuley and that snake of a hotel clerk. My kidnapping was set up by them for sure.'

'I think you're right,' Jim said, looking westwards. 'Trinity Creek is where we'll go. Waldrop's dead. That score is settled. My job is gone, along with Palmito. And Lena-Marie, who was my' – he gulped – 'friend, is gone, too.'

Several days later, as they rode into the town's outskirts, they came across a small party of mourners leaving the Trinity Creek cemetery.

The medico, John G. Brandon, pulled at the reins of the black in the shafts of his spring buggy, holding them breast-high with one hand. He took off his black hat and lowered his head awkwardly.

'Why, Mrs Harrison, I'm afraid you've gotten here a mite too late. . . . We didn't know you were coming. I would have delayed the funeral and the burying if I'd been told.'

'Delayed. . .? A funeral? What do you mean, Doctor?' Alice's voice was sharp with sudden dread.

'I'm sorry to have to shock you, ma'am, but Mr

Harrison is dead.'

'Dead! But Matt was recovering from his injuries, improving. What happened?'

Doc Brandon shook his white head sadly.

'So sorry, Mrs Harrison. . . . It was me who found him when I visited. He'd gone back to the Double H and shot himself.'

Jim pulled his horse close to Alice's and put out a hand to steady her.

'Matt shot himself! For God's sake why?'

Brandon gave it to them quickly, which in a long and rugged career was as mercifully as he'd learned how.

'There was a shooting ruckus in town. Alexander McAuley and his – ah – woman died. Matt got back to the ranch, where he came to his senses after a fashion but was overcome by his old melancholia. He left a note. Said he couldn't face the fact his miserable, ruined life would now finish at the end of a hangman's rope. So he ended it his own way.'

Alice went ashen. 'Oh, poor Matt! That's awful.'

'Hellish,' Jim murmured. 'McAuley was a scoundrel who deserved to die, but Matt Harrison didn't, whatever his faults.'

But somehow the ghastly news, when Alice and Jim had reflected on it, didn't seem such a huge surprise. The train of events, as they found out over the subsequent days, had had a doom-laden inevitability.

Many weeks later, Jim said to Alice, 'I'd like to rebuild the Double H for you, for Matt's memory . . . for us.'

'Do you think you could?' she said.

'Sure. It's high time we made something of our lives.'

She looked him straight in the eye and said earnestly, 'I'd like to share the Double H with you, Jim.'

'You would? Why—' As though the thought had only just occurred to him, he said, 'Do you reckon you might get fond enough of me to marry me?'

'I've always been fond enough of you for that, Jim. Must we continue acting like we're polite acquaintances, that we've never been friends, never kissed before?'

'Not any longer!' Jim said emphatically. 'There's been too much misery, too much dying. It's high time we made a new life.'

He took her in his arms. It had cost a peck of blood and suffering, but Jim and Alice had won their peace.